CHILDREN OF STARDUST

EDUDZI ADODO

CHILDREN OF STARDUST

ACCORD BOOKS

Norton Young Readers

An Imprint of W. W. Norton & Company
Independent Publishers Since 1923

To my mother, Ketline

For information about permission to reproduce selections from this book,
write to Permissions, W. W. Norton & Company, Inc.,
500 Fifth Avenue, New York, NY 10110

For information about special discounts for bulk purchases, please contact
W. W. Norton Special Sales at specialsales@wwnorton.com or 800-233-4830

Manufacturing by Lake Book Manufacturing
Book design by Hana Anouk Nakamura
Production manager: Julia Druskin

ISBN 978-1-324-03077-5

W. W. Norton & Company, Inc., 500 Fifth Avenue, New York, N.Y. 10110
www.wwnorton.com

W. W. Norton & Company Ltd., 15 Carlisle Street, London W1D 3BS

1 2 3 4 5 6 7 8 9 0

CHILDREN OF STARDUST

MEET THE CHARACTERS

ZERO
Home planet: **ANANSI 12**

Affiliation: **SHANGO HEART**

Likes: **SABA FACTS, AFROBEATS MUSIC, EXPANDING HIS ZERO WORRIES BUSINESS**

KOBASTICKERS:

JUPITER

CABBAGENIX

DEGIZZENOUVOX

CAMIH
Home planet: **GANTINIA**

Affiliation: **SHANGO HEART**

Likes: **ADVENTURES, PRANKS, PEOPLE THAT PIQUE HER CURIOSITY**

KOBASTICKERS:

BLUEFLASH   LIGHTORBNIX

LADYBUG   REDUCENIX

LADI
Home planet: **TITANIUS**

Affiliation: **SHANGO HEART**.

Likes: **WHIZZERS, PRANKS, BEING POPULAR**

KOBASTICKERS:

CUREX   RADYONDELNIX

ZOUTIVOLE

WANDERBLATCH
Home planet: **SCOOBADI**

Affiliation: **HOUSE OF JUPITER**

Likes: **ROASTED CATERPILLARS**

KOBASTICKERS:

FLEAREPELNIX

CHENIPLATENIX

LENOIR
Home Planet: **RED GRAVA**

Affiliation: **NONE (FREELANCE BOUNTY HUNTER)**

Likes: **MONEY, RARE KOBASTICKERS**

KOBASTICKERS:

BLACKFLASH

OCTAVE
Home planet: **SOL**

Affiliation: **SHANGO HEART**

Likes: **MUSIC, OLD SPACE ELF SONGS, ANCIENT GREMLIN BALLADS, POETRY**

KOBASTICKERS:

ORPHEUS MUSICSHEETNIX

HELPNIX

MR. GAUCHE
Home planet: **PLEXUS**

Affiliation: **SHANGO HEART, COUNCIL OF GUILDMASTERS**

Likes: **ARTIFACTS FROM BLUE, SHANGO HEART PRIDE**

KOBASTICKERS:

MANOFTHEHOUR GOLDFLASH

REKIPERGANE

EFUA
Home planet: **ANANSI 12**

Affiliation: **VIPERKINGS**

Likes: **SABINA KANO
LUXURY BRAND
CLOTHES**

KOBASTICKERS:

BLUEFLASH   LINGUANIX

KANOLIKSNIX

KHABIB
Home planet: **BRISCA 9**

Affiliation: **SCORPIODUKES**

Likes: **HIP-HOP MUSIC**

KOBASTICKERS:

LUPUS

VUWA-MODNIX

ROZAN
Home planet: **MARS 22**

Affiliation: **LEOMBRE FAMILY
(SPACE MAFIA)**

Likes: **CRIMINAL ACTIVITY**

KOBASTICKERS:

ANDROMEDA

BLACKFLASH

CHAPTER 1

ZERO was on his way to the crash site of the whizzer he had seen falling from the sky when he heard someone yell:

"Y-your money or y-your life!"

Zero raised his hands in the air, causing a few packets of plantain chips to tumble to the desert ground.

In his head, Zero made a quick inventory of everything he had on him. As always, the oversized brown coat he wore whenever he rescued stranded space travelers bulged with enough food to feed a small army of space trolls. The inner pockets were filled to the brim with packets of Jabba sweet-and-sour roasted cricket snacks. He had a slab of Dralaxian blue cheese whose smell caused most creatures with two nostrils and a working nervous system to give him a wide berth. Going down his right pant leg he had some ostrich meat sausages, and going down his left he had a Komodo and lettuce sandwich that folded over his knee every time he took a step.

In his knapsack, he had a first aid kit and a Goober—a portable computer that allowed stranded space travelers to make emergency calls, for a fee. He also had a huge condor bone for Fido, the guardian of the Temple of Ifanabe. This bandit would most certainly not be interested in that. But then there was the gold medallion shaped like a comb that he wore under the blue kente bandanna wrapped around his neck. The medallion was a gift from Zoe, his mentor and favorite person in the galaxy. The bandanna was the only thing he had from his mother. He also had his white-and-blue Abalo 12 sneakers, and he would fight if the bandit tried to take those!

"Can we talk about this?" asked Zero.

The voice seemed to consider it.

"N-no?" said the voice uncertainly.

Zero chanced a glance at his adversary.

To his right, the barrel of a hunting rifle poked out from over a boulder and winked at him in the early morning sunlight. Even from this distance he could clearly see the barrel was shaking.

"Bo, is that you?" said Zero.

"Who's asking?"

"It's me."

"You who?"

"Zero, you dummy."

A head popped out over the top of the boulder. Most of it was hidden by aviator goggles and a great deal of bandages. It was topped by leather flaps styled like bunny ears. He looked like a mummified rabbit.

"How do I know you're really Zero and not some desert will-o'-the-wisp taking the form of Zero?"

"That's actually a good point. You could take my word for it, or you could come check for yourself?"

Bo thought this through.

"Fine. But don't move a muscle."

Bo's head disappeared, and a few moments later he looped

around the boulder. When he was about a foot from Zero, Bo fished inside his pocket and pulled out a hideous pair of spectacles, placed them clumsily on his face, and squinted at Zero.

"Zero! It really is you!" said Bo.

"I know," said Zero.

Bo threw his rifle aside and hugged Zero. Then he froze.

"What's that smell?" said Bo, sniffing the air.

"Dralaxian blue cheese," said Zero, untangling himself from Bo's embrace. "Bo, what did I tell you about being friendly with your targets?"

Bo smiled sheepishly.

"You're right, Zero!" he said, fumbling for the rifle he had dropped.

"Of course I am. Secondly, you should always wear your glasses. You know you can't see without them—you're holding your rifle the wrong way around, by the way."

"Sorry!" said Bo, turning the gun so the barrel was once more facing Zero.

"Thirdly, when you're ambushing someone, you need to project confidence. Your tone and body language are important. Stand up straight. Don't stammer. Don't be indecisive, and definitely don't hug people."

With every piece of advice, Bo's head drooped a bit more. His shoulders sagged, and the barrel of his gun sank lower and lower like a wilting flower.

"I'll never be a good desert bandit, Zero! I'm terrible at this!"

"You're being harsh on yourself. You've made a lot of

strides. Besides, why would your brothers leave you out here on ambush duty all alone if they didn't trust you?"

"You think so?" asked Bo brightly.

Zero winced. The Desert Bunnies were a gang of bandits who roamed around the Ankobi Desert and were famous for their bunny-themed attire and their formidable propensity for friendly fire. The Desert Bunnies were a family business, but Bo was so clumsy that his brothers had probably stationed him here hoping he would get eaten by a Komodo dragon or one of the giant condors that lived on the abandoned satellite field nearby.

Aloud Zero said, "S-sure. You just need to stick with it."

"Thanks, Zero. You really know how to cheer a person up. I don't know how I would manage without you. Don't know why I was worrying so much . . ."

"Exactly. Unfortunately for you, I don't have anything valuable on me, but I think I saw a Kundabian merchant heading this way," said Zero confidentially. It was a lie of course; he had not seen anyone behind him.

"A Kundabian merchant? They're always loaded with money!" said Bo, jumping up and down in excitement. "My brothers never let me stick up Kundabian merchants. They are always leaving me with desert trolls. And they almost never travel without their Brutus cards."

The Brutus card was used by merchants traveling through the desert. When approached by desert bandits, cardholders were exempt from being mugged. It was one of the benefits of the unionization of bandits in the Ankobi Desert. Cardholders paid monthly contributions and in return could only be subjected to a maximum of four muggings a year (down from the customary hundred or so), which they could schedule in advance for convenience. Cardholders also had access to premium services such as first aid after a mugging and bandits who said "Fanks" and "Pweez."

Zero had one too, but was behind on payments so technically it was expired.

"Now is your big chance. Why don't you get back to your position and get ready for your next target?" prodded Zero.

"Yes of course! Gee, thanks, Zero!"

Bo made a great show of returning to his station, and once again took up position behind his boulder with his hunting rifle scanning the desert.

As Zero walked away, he could hear Bo reciting Zero's advice over and over again, until his voice faded into the desert.

Zero walked for a good half hour looking for the crashed spaceship. The air visibly shook with the heat, and he had to squint from the glare of the sun.

Zero was beginning to think he had gotten his directions all wrong when he noticed plumes of dark black smoke in the distance, rising toward the powder blue sky.

He broke into a short jog. When he reached the lip of a crater, he looked down and whistled.

Great sheets of billowing smoke rose from the wreckage of a whizzer crash.

Zero had seen many whizzers—personal spaceships that had revolutionized space travel. Most had outlandish appearances (Lady Melia, the number seven Saba in the galaxy, had a whizzer fashioned like a rabbit with sunglasses, and Zero remembered reading about an award-winning whizzer that had been designed to look like a germ).

This one was no different. Through the flames he could make out a roof fashioned in the shape of a giant furry head. The front of the car formed a snout that had been flattened by the collision, and the front grilles were fashioned like teeth.

The wreckage looked like a yeti with a head injury.

The sand around the base of the wreckage was scorched, and the combined smell of gasoline and smoke stung his nostrils.

Zero walked down the side of the crater to get a closer look. Heat rolled out from the wreckage, making his eyes water.

All around him, stony outcrops carved by the wind looked like hundreds of apple cores dropped onto the desert. Overhead, desert condors greased the skies on silent wings. As they flew directly above him, one went rigid and tumbled out of the sky, crashing into a sand dune in a puff of feathers. The others gave cries of alarm and glared at Zero.

"Sorry," said Zero, pulling the zipper of his coat all the way up to his chin. He added to himself, "I really should do something about this cheese . . ."

Looking down, he noticed deep footprints that led away from the wreckage up the flank of the crater.

Zero followed them out of the crater and a little ways across the desert before he paused.

The footprints were heading to the Temple of Ifanabe.

The Temple of Ifanabe was carved out of a boulder the size of a small hill. It was sculpted in the shape of the head of one of the Adeshas, the daughters of the King of the Galaxy. It had two gaping holes for eyes, which always gave Zero the impression of someone glaring at him from a distance. A ring of cacti dappled with violet and yellow flowers ran around the outside of the temple.

Zero slipped inside the temple just as a strong breeze sent sand pelting against the mouth of the cave. Once inside, he was grateful for the cool shade, which offered relief from the bruising sunlight.

The museum had been named in honor of the Adesha Ifanabe, one of the biggest patrons of Sabas in the galaxy. The lobby of the temple doubled as a museum dedicated to Saba history.

Sabas, of course, were licensed adventurers. In the olden days, they were sworn to protect the galactic royal family, but now they spent their days exploring space, retrieving lost treasures, and chasing criminals. They wielded Kobastickers, adhesive objects made of Koba energy, which granted their wearers magical abilities. There were Kobastickers that allowed you to talk to birds, or levitate objects. There were even some that made you turn anything you touched into fried plantain.

Sabas were revered and loved, and most were incredibly rich. They were also free. They could go anywhere in the galaxy and live their lives as they saw fit, and that was what Zero admired most about them.

It was Zero's dream to become a Saba. But for that he would need to join one of the dozens of Saba guilds in his sector of the galaxy.

Zero made his way through the lobby.

He knew all the exhibits by heart.

The "Wonderful Whizzers" exhibit was displayed inside a cracked and dirty glass cabinet. It was a bust of Kola Oguku, the inventor of the very first whizzer. A picture showed a chubby man with a long, flowing white robe, white sneakers, and a handlebar mustache standing with a hand on his invention—the very first whizzer. It was called *Pamplemousse I*, and it looked like an orange on wheels.

But his favorite exhibit was "The Hero with No Name and the Zodiac Twelve." Cordoned off by mouse-eaten velvet ropes were sculpted statues of the twelve Zodiac Sabas and their leader, the Hero with No Name. Many years ago, the Hero with No Name and the legendary twelve Sabas, each possessing one of the twelve Kobastickers named after the zodiac signs, banded together to stop Zomon the Dark King from conquering the galaxy. They defeated him and his army of Dark Sabas led by the Seven Sins—generals who each wielded a Kobasticker named after the cardinal sins. The Hero with No Name and the Zodiac Twelve then trapped Zomon and his generals in a remote realm called the Oblong Dimension.

Zero often came to the Temple whenever he was frustrated with Jude, the ruler of the City of Children.

The temple was in disrepair, most of the glass displays were smashed, and the artifacts were covered in thick layers of dust (and some bat droppings), but to Zero they could not have been more impressive.

He sometimes closed his eyes and imagined the room brimming with visitors admiring pristine exhibits.

Other times, he wandered around the temple imagining he was a scientist testing the first whizzer, or one of the Zodiac Sabas facing off against Zomon. Like a chameleon moving through a jungle, the content of his fantasies would shift and change to fit the different exhibits he walked past.

As he meandered through the exhibits, following the trail of footprints, Zero heard the high-pitched squeals of Goymons. The mischievous little two-tailed monkeys with light brown fur and black faces peered at him from holes in the walls.

But there was another sound, like something big trying to be stealthy: heavy, padded footsteps. The noise stopped whenever he stopped, and resumed when Zero continued to walk. Once or twice, out of the corner of his eye, he would see a giant shadow towering over the display cases.

Zero smiled.

He walked down an aisle of glass cabinets filled with Saba artifacts. As he reached the end, quick as a coyote he looped around to the aisle on his right.

"Got you, Fido!"

Sure enough, the temple's guardian loomed before Zero, frozen mid-stride. He was so tall his head brushed against the top of the chamber.

Fido was a dog-like creature that looked like a giant mop fitted with an overbite and a drooling mouth. His eyes were hidden behind a curtain of blue fur so dirty that when he shook himself, the air was instantly thick with clouds of dust.

His bushy tail thudded excitedly against the ground, making the floor of the chamber shake.

Zero still remembered the first day he had come face-to-face with Fido. He had been terrified as the giant creature appeared before him, his bulk blocking out the light in the chamber. But he had not eaten Zero, and in exchange Zero brought him food every time he came to the temple. Fido had been abandoned on the planet by a space traveler, and as an orphan, Zero felt a type of kinship with him. They had become good friends.

Zero opened his knapsack and pulled out a giant condor bone wrapped in brown paper, and dropped it at Fido's feet.

"There you go, big man. I have a little task I need to accomplish, so I'll see you later."

Zero patted Fido's forearm before following the mysterious footsteps deeper into the temple.

Zero was very careful as he made his way. The temple had been built with booby traps to ward off enemies. Over the years, Zero had memorized which tiles to walk on and which paths to take. Once, when he was younger, he lost focus for a split second and stepped on a tile that set off a trap. He had spent the next twenty seconds running at the speed of light to dodge half a dozen poisoned darts released from openings in the walls.

To Zero's astonishment, the space traveler had taken the

exact path to avoid all the traps. And then the footprints disappeared right in the middle of the hall.

"Is anybody here?" he called loudly, his words echoing down the corridor.

No one replied.

Zero decided to have a look in a few chambers. If he didn't find the stranded traveler, then at least he would go home knowing that he had given it his best shot.

He looked in the first chamber on his right. It was empty.

Next, he tried the chamber on the opposite side of the corridor, but that too was empty.

Zero was already a few feet inside the third chamber when he noticed the figure looming beside the entrance.

There was a flutter of movement, and Zero felt two fingers grip his neck with a hold like the bite of a crocodile. He froze, like a rabbit caught in a snare.

A cold voice said, "No sudden moves, kid! Not unless you have a death wish."

CHAPTER 2

"**HERE** is the situation. I currently have two fingers wrapped around your throat. I bet you want to ask, Why is that important? Well, I'll tell you. I have a special ability that allows me to manipulate electricity. The strength of the charge I release depends on a number of factors. Ten, to be precise. Essentially, the number of fingers that I have in contact with a surface at any point in time. With me so far?"

Zero nodded.

"Excellent. Right now, with two fingers, you should be feeling mild discomfort and a little current flowing through your body. If I were to apply another, however . . ."

The man pressed a third finger against Zero's throat.

Instantly, Zero felt a charge course through his body. His muscles contracted painfully and his teeth jammed together with an audible click. A rush of electricity passed through his brain, rising in intensity as if an invisible dial were being turned up from one to ten.

The man removed his finger and Zero felt his whole body go limp.

"You will have experienced muscle spasms and brain freezes with three fingers. Now, if I were to use four fingers—"

"Don't use four fingers!" pleaded Zero.

"Smart man. Four fingers would be the point of no return.

We would be talking about a heart attack. So now that I have your attention, I want you to listen very carefully. Nod to me if you understand."

Zero nodded once more. His gaze fell on a tomb in the center of the room, and he blanched. He hoped he wasn't going to end up alongside its current occupant.

"Music to my ears! Now, I am going to ask you a few questions and I want you to answer as truthfully as possible. If I get even the slightest impression you are lying to me, I might just have to fry your brains. Understood?"

Again, Zero nodded.

"Are you in league with Lenoir?" the voice demanded.

"I don't even know who that is!"

"Good. Are you a quillux?"

"A quillux?" Zero asked, confused.

"Foul demon creatures that take the shape of children until they sneeze and become fourteen-foot-tall beasts that can punch holes through reinforced Plutonian concrete."

"No, I'm not a quillux."

"You're not a private detective sent by my ex-wife to—"

"No, I'm not!"

"Alright, alright, just checking. You know you can never be too careful in my line of business!"

Zero heard him sniff the air.

"What's that smell?" the voice grunted.

"Dralaxian blue cheese."

"Well, it smells like death's underpants. Now you listen here, I'm going to release you, but I want you to remember the feeling of my fingers across your throat. Know that my ability is not just effective when I touch things. I can zap things from a distance too."

Zero felt the man's hold relax, and he stumbled forward, clutching his throat.

He turned to look at the man and started.

Zero was staring at a tall creature the size of a bear and covered in white fur. It had a snout like a pig and two canines that jutted out from under its lower lip. It had deep-set yellow eyes with piercing blue irises, like the little crystals mined on the surface of Neptune 4. It wore a black-and-white-striped shirt like a prisoner.

The creature barely registered Zero's shock. It began to pace with its hands behind its back, mumbling things under its breath.

"What mess have you found yourself in Wander . . . I don't have much time . . . How will I find a worthy successor . . . ?"

A thought dropped into Zero's mind.

"You're the one who arrived in the whizzer!" he exclaimed.

The beast stopped pacing and looked at him.

"Perhaps I am. Why?" asked the beast.

Zero stood up straight and cleared his throat. This was an excellent opportunity to try out his new sales pitch.

"Perfect, because I came to help you. I own a rescue company, see," said Zero, beaming. He held up his backpack, as if that would settle the matter.

"A rescue company?" asked the beast.

Zero nodded. "That's right. Zero Worries. We specialize in assisting stranded space travelers."

Zero fumbled inside his coat and pulled out a tattered flyer. He made a vain attempt to smooth it out and then handed it to the beast.

"Have you heard of Bobby Adjanke?" asked Zero.

The beast shook his head.

"He was a bank robber. He crashed out here while running away from the Space Force. I helped get him some disguises and a phone call to his associates. What about Linda Maloune?"

The beast shook his head again.

This was going badly. Talking with the beast was like adding milk to a cup of black coffee that never grows lighter. He was a black hole impervious to Zero's commercial arguments and natural charms, but Zero did not despair.

"It doesn't really matter. What matters is I offer three tiers of services: Scorpion, Viper, and Komodo. With the Scorpion option for 30.99 berries, you get the standard rescue, food, and drinks package with a five-minute phone call to anywhere in the galaxy—toll charges apply. The Viper option gets you all that and a tour of the Ifanabe temple as well as a three-day pass that exempts you from muggings by the Desert Bunnies and having your whizzer ransacked for parts. Now, with the Komodo option—my personal favorite—you get all the above, plus whizzer repair and maintenance, daily massages, unlimited access to the Goober, a VIP visit to the City of Children, disguises, and legal representation."

Which was not technically true. For legal representation, he depended on Jim McCray, an old hermit who used to be a member of the Intergalactic Bar Association and now worked for the Space Mafia. He got cursed by one of his clients (a space witch) after he lost a case, and now spent most of his days thinking he was a Plutonian bullfrog. His availability was hit or miss.

The Komodo option was the best value for customers, but Zero's least profitable option since it involved outsourcing a lot of the work. Not to mention the criminal exposure. Dirty Bottoms was a Desert Bunny who would often extort Zero in return for his services, but he did cook incredibly well.

"How much would it cost for you to be quiet?"

Zero did some rough calculations with his fingers but stopped when he caught sight of the beast's fiery gaze.

"Just kidding, boss." Zero chuckled halfheartedly. "For you, I can do that for free."

"Good. Do you have any food?" the beast asked.

A customer request! This was something Zero could work with. He opened his knapsack. The beast watched him hungrily as he pulled out packets of food.

"How much?" asked the beast.

"2.99 berries..."—the beast held his thumb and his index finger a few inches apart, a spark playing in the space between—"but I'll give you these as a free sample," Zero added quickly.

"How nice of you," he said, taking the packets from Zero.

"Anything to make a customer happy," Zero replied, laughing hollowly.

It would be hard for Zero to ever save enough money to pay for his Saba guild applications under these circumstances.

He made quick calculations in his head and reasoned that he could get by with offering two packets for free. But the beast had collected five packets of Komodo jerky and half a dozen cricket snacks. Zero sighed as he pictured his profits dwindling.

The beast helped himself to the packets of food with a ferocity that made Zero flinch.

Zero knew a lost cause when he saw one. He sighed, and was turning around to leave when he noticed a briefcase leaning against the entrance, and a small pyramid-shaped object that had fallen out of it. As Zero got closer he saw it was black but had intricate thunderbolt designs on each side. It was scratched and chipped from years of usage.

Zero turned and looked at the beast, who was popping cricket snacks into his mouth, packaging and all.

"Sir, I think you may have forgotten this—" began Zero as he reached down and grabbed hold of the pyramid.

His hand felt as if it was being welded to it. Zero watched with growing amazement as caterpillars of light crawled across his hand. He winced as he felt a current enter his skin and flow up his arm like magma sluicing through his veins.

There was a blazing flash and Zero was blasted backward as if he had been shoved in the chest by a space troll. He collapsed on the floor.

Zero's skin prickled with sweat. He clutched his right elbow with his left hand. His arm felt like cold vapor was blowing through his bone marrow. He looked up at the beast and found his confusion mirrored perfectly on its face. The two yellow orbs of its eyes grew big like the lights of an oncoming train.

The beast stared at Zero as if seeing him for the first time. He looked from the pyramid to Zero and back again several times before rushing to Zero's side.

"Your arms," the beast commanded. "Show me."

Zero held them out.

The beast grabbed his right wrist and peeled back his sleeve.

Glowing on his forearm was a strange symbol.

It was in the shape of an oval, and showed a planet with orange and purple streaks and a thunderbolt at its center. Around the planet was a great ring.

A Kobasticker.

Somewhere outside the temple there came a rumble that quickly turned into a roar. The building shook, causing sand to trickle down from the ceiling. Then, as quickly as it had started, the chaos stopped, leaving the temple eerily quiet.

"We don't have time. It must be *him*. He must have followed me to this planet," the beast said urgently. "Go! He must not find you here!" He pushed Zero toward the hall.

Zero scrambled to his feet, his heart beating wildly in his chest. "I, er . . . I'll be seeing you around," he said, backing away still clutching his forearm.

Zero turned and ran and did not stop until he had made it out of the temple. Outside, the sky was dappled with fleecy clouds and a delicious breeze swept over his body. The circular shadows of a few vultures swept over the sand. Zero hurried home, toward the City of Children, constantly darting looks over his shoulder, half expecting the beast to chase after him.

CHAPTER 3

ZERO was halfway to the City of Children when the spasms began. Electric charges surged through him, causing every muscle in his body to contract, as if someone had pressed a live wire against his tongue. The pain made his head throb and his eyes water, but it subsided for a moment as he reached the digging site.

Massive holes dotted the landscape like pockmarks. Many had been dug by the children under orders from Jude, the ruler of Cégolim. Jude's uncle, the previous mayor, had believed that a group of pilgrims to the Temple of Ifanabe had hidden treasure in the area surrounding the City of Children. His father had been obsessed with finding it, so when the adults all disappeared after the Great Flash, Jude picked up the search.

Cégolim, the City of Children, was an ancient city carved into a giant outcrop the shape of a horseshoe. It used to be a holy city built by pilgrims and worshippers of Ifanabe. But it had changed since the Great Flash.

Some of the children were old enough to remember it. One morning, a blinding light filled the sky. When it subsided, all the adults were gone—leaving the children all alone.

Zero passed through the giant archway that was the entrance to the City of Children. In the past, Jude's underlings would have been on patrol, guarding the wall. But that was in the early days after the adults left. Now, the cords of discipline binding Jude's underlings had snapped and they rarely came this way.

Inside the walls, the old town spread out in front of Zero, made of clay buildings decorated with elaborate red markings that had long since turned brown. The children had abandoned these many years ago. After the euphoria of being free of the adults had subsided, the children quickly realized that running a town was harder than they'd expected. They'd retreated to a smaller area they were sure they could maintain.

Still, signs of careless management abounded. Cégolim was a city managed by children—impatient and careless, and who never built or repaired anything, but rather used things until they broke down. The city naturally began to deteriorate under their lazy care, and now litter lined the streets and broken furniture was stacked haphazardly outside huts.

It was early afternoon, and so by now most of the children would have been away on the new digging sites that were behind the city.

Zero passed by Fools' Yard—a pair of wooden pens built side by side in the center of Cégolim's main square. It was for citizens who didn't dig well enough or who had been responsible for such offenses as sleeping during one of Jude's weekly addresses, not laughing enough at one of his stories, or else laughing a bit too hard. Children who upset Jude were branded with an ink stamp and had to show up at Fools' Yard the following day. It was the most popular form of entertainment in the city. Jude's boys and other bored citizens would watch as punished children took turns wearing Mr. Scratchy (a moldy cotton shirt full of mites that when worn felt like strapping on a beehive) or took care of Bolger, a temperamental blue boarhound who spent most of his time running over children who entered his enclosure.

Zero also went by the Tree of Bob. It was an old star willow tree that had withered and died. Over the years, children had slipped their parents' clothes onto the low-lying branches. Once all the spots were taken, they had begun to nail pieces to the bark. The children would come and pray under the tree, hoping that one day their parents would return to save them.

Zero's home was nestled in one of the cliff faces overlooking the center of town. He climbed the steep path and entered through a narrow entrance, keeping to the side of the corridor to avoid the piles of sand that poured out of the open rooms like unfurled brown tongues.

Zero's room was just what you would have expected from a hard-core Saba fan. His walls were plastered with pictures of famous Sabas and rare luxury whizzers. An assortment of objects and trinkets lined his shelves—gifts from stranded space travelers to thank him for his assistance.

Zero hurriedly took off his backpack and coat, packets of food spilling onto the hard stone floor. Zero had never heard of a Kobasticker attaching to a person against their will. He worried there was some dark magic afoot.

Zero tried to scrape the Kobasticker off, but there were no edges or seams that he could lift. He might as well have peeled off his skin. He then tried running some water over it, and nearly passed out from the shock of electricity when the gush from the tap hit his forearm.

Zero pulled out his Goober from his backpack. It was a perfectly square blue cube with golden moldings. He pressed a button on the side of the cube, and it unfurled like a water lily to reveal a miniature tree. From the top grew a large flower with beautiful yellow petals, and in the center of the flower was a glass prism. The prism began to glow as an image was projected in midair above the Goober.

IDENTIFICATION REQUIRED.

This was the part Zero dreaded. One of the annoying things about Goobers was that they were very secure and required nasal verification. To verify a person's identity, tweezers would pull hair from your nostrils for analysis, and only if it matched the owner would it open up. As bad as it sounds, the actual experience was infinitely worse. Zero looked forward to the day he would have enough money to buy the newer model, which had fingerprint verification—the Goooober.

He watched as two gray tendrils slid out from the base of the tree. Zero leaned down and shut his eyes. He felt the tweezers ram into his right nostril, then a painful yank as it pulled out a hair. He clapped a hand over his nose and fought the urge to sneeze. A few moments later, words appeared on the screen above the Goober.

WELCOME ZERO.

The words disappeared and the screen changed to his home page.

Over two dozen roots curled out from the base of the Goober. They all ended in neat little squares on which letters were imprinted. There was even a thin root ending in a large bulb you could use to navigate a cursor on the Goober screen.

It was hard for him to type anything with the spasms.

"Chuksapanza," he grumbled as his fingers shook. His eyes went cross-eyed and he felt a painful tree of electricity bloom within him. A pair of pigeons standing on the ledge of his window looked on with rapt attention.

Eventually he managed to load Meebo, the search engine. First, he tried to identify his Kobasticker. He ran his arm over his Goober's scanner, but the Goober's search came back with a *No matches found*. Zero felt a throb of panic. This made no sense. Perhaps this Kobasticker was faulty? Or worse yet, perhaps it was a fake?

He typed: *Kobasticker problems, consequences of a fake Kobasticker that does not come off*.

He opened the first search result and scanned the article. He read *gruesome death* and *permanent* three times in one paragraph and almost passed out.

He got up and half ran, half stumbled into the bathroom.

Once he was inside, he leaned against the door and let himself slide down onto his heels. Zero stared at his hands. They were shaking, and little bolts of light crawled all over them. Strange symbols played across his vision, and his eyes pricked as if he had rubbed pepper in them. He struggled to his feet and looked at himself in the mirror. A thin boy stared back at him, with cropped hair and a blue bandanna tied around his neck. An X-shaped scar ran down his right cheek. For a split second, a spark ran across his eye and his irises turned blue with golden thunderbolts inside them.

What is happening to me?

There was a roaring in Zero's ears and he shut his eyes tightly. He felt a cold wind blowing around him, and then, all at once, it stopped. Zero opened his eyes and stared at his reflection. His eyes had returned to their normal shape and color.

Zero let himself slide onto the floor. He fell into a short doze, but woke up when he heard a few notes of a familiar tune floating through the bathroom door.

It was his Goober. He had set an alarm for *Saba Now*.

The spasms seemed to have subsided.

For a moment, Zero thought about his future. It would be hard for him to run a thriving business if he spent the rest of his life as a walking short-circuit.

He checked his arm, and was surprised to see that the Kobasticker had begun to blur around the edges. With any luck, it was beginning to fade away.

Zero stumbled out of the bathroom room and walked over to his Goober. There were fifteen minutes left until the start of *Saba Now*. Enough time for Zero to check his emails.

Zero plopped onto his bed and logged on to his Sigmia account. Everyone in the galaxy used the social network, even some of the Desert Bunnies. It wasn't unusual for Zero to get mugged only to get a friend request from his assailant when he got home.

As always, the first thing he did was check his inbox for messages from Zoe.

There were none. Wherever she was, Zero hoped that she was okay.

Next, he checked his email and braced himself.

Zero had sent dozens of requests to join Saba guilds—a necessary step if you hadn't been scouted. With this latest batch, he had sent emails to three hundred Saba guilds over the years. None had replied favorably so far.

He opened the first email. It was from a popular guild called the Titanhearts.

Dear Zero,

It is with great sadness that we announce that we are unable to accept your application to join the Titanheart Guild. Though we were touched by your motivation letter and your story, the video footage you sent us did not prove you have sufficient proficiency at using Kobastickers to justify acceptance to our guild.

We expected proof that you can levitate an object three feet in the air without assistance . . .

Zero winced.

To prove Koba proficiency, Zero was expected to make a bottle of water rise off a table. In his video submission, he had managed to make the bottle shake, but that had been because he was kicking the table with his foot.

. . . As a result, we must reject your application. We would, however, be glad to receive another application from you in the following cycle as long as you use one of the accepted types of Kobastickers to perform your proof of Koba proficiency. We thank you for your interest in the Titanheart Guild.

Zero groaned. The only Kobastickers he could find were low grade and defective. He bought them off a shady character called Mr. Trix who Zero widely suspected sold goblin-made Kobasticker imitations.

He looked at the other emails. As he'd expected, they were mostly rejection letters:

... Mermaid Crown is only open to members who possess water-type Kobastickers. We wish you well in your search for a Saba guild.

We would be glad to accept a future application, should you obtain a water-type Kobasticker and fulfill the criteria for selection ...

And:

Dear Applicant,

Just a reminder that Scavenger King is only open to GOBLINS. Though you did make a hearty attempt, your feet were visible in the photograph you sent us.

Zero blew air into his cheeks at his own lack of attention to detail.

It was almost 4 p.m. He logged off and went to the *Saba Now* web page.

Saba Now analyzed the latest news and rumors in the world of Sabas. There were often dozens of useful tips and testimonies of Sabas who'd managed to get recruited by a guild. Zero never missed an episode.

The Goober screen turned dark and the words *Saba Now* appeared in dazzling gold letters.

A few moments later, the scene changed and he was looking at two elves, each wearing an oversized shirt with the words *Saba Now* on them. The one to the left had red hair and freckles, and the one to the left had violet hair and wore glasses.

As the show started, Zero rushed over to his backpack to grab a carton of mango juice and some popcorn, making sure to pay himself for the goods before rushing back to sit down just as the theme song ended.

"*Good morning, ladies and gentlemen. May the light of Ifanabe be upon you,*" said the redheaded elf, using the traditional Saba greeting. "*I'm Banzo and this is Kanjo, and welcome to another Saba Now episode, where, as always, we will be giving you the very latest in the world of Sabas. Today's episode has been brought to you by Burgess & Sons, famous Kobastickers repairers. They are sponsoring our special raffle, where we will be giving listeners a chance to win a rare Kobasticker—the Poseidon from the Titan series. All you need to do is correctly answer the question of the day and this prized Kobasticker could be yours. Now onto our news, as we have quite a lot to talk about.*"

"*Yes we do, Banzo,*" the violet-haired elf replied. "*We will first talk about the mysterious art thief Erena Rosamond. Viewers will remember we spoke about her last week.*

"*Rosamond has claimed to have been behind a number of incredible art heists. The only problem is, the purported victims have always denied that they had anything stolen from them. Rosamond claims there has been a smear campaign against her, as many of her recent purported heists have gone unreported or been flatly denied by art galleries. An annoying situation for the thief, who finds herself unable to prove she has stolen the* artifacts. So: Erena Rosamond—genius thief or attention-seeking whiner? We will be having an exclusive interview with the gentlewoman thief, who will tell us how the smear campaign is affecting her mental health as well as her standing in the thief world."

Banzo continued, "Now for the latest Saba guild rankings, published by the Intergalactic Saba Organization just this morning. The Lionheart Guild stays firmly in the number one spot. But Eclipse Noir is steadily rising in the ranks, and we have a new entry into the Top Ten and some dramatic changes, including updates on the lawsuits against Shango Heart, the fan-favorite guild, for destruction of property. Don't go anywhere!"

"But first, we have a public service announcement," Kanjo interjected. "Attempts continue to locate the party of Sabas sent to explore the Dark Galaxy. The Intergalactic Saba Organization still has hopes that it will get news from the expedition."

Zero felt as if his heart were being wrung out like a wet towel.

He still remembered reading about it in *Saba World* magazine. Zoe had been selected to head the expedition. He had felt so proud of her. There had been a whole *Saba Now* episode dedicated to the launch. The president of the Intergalactic Saba Organization, as well as many heads of planets, had gathered to celebrate the launch.

"It will now be nine hundred and forty days since we last connected with the expedition, which contained some of our most distinguished Sabas. The infamous Dark Galaxy is believed to be the source of Koba, the life energy that forms the basis of Kobastickers.

"The expedition was headed by Zoe "Stormfox" Sitso, the freedom fighter and rogue who traversed much of our galaxy with her now-deceased boyfriend Kadj. Zoe was a former number one Saba and one of the wielders of the twelve legendary Zodiac Kobastickers. Readers may remember them as the heroes who banded together to defeat Zomon the Dark King and save the galaxy. Zoe was also voted the Most Beautiful Saba in the Galaxy six times, not to mention she was a Saba of the Century Award winner.

"We still hold out hope for the members of the expedition. Now stay tuned, we have much more Saba news to tell you after the break. Here is the latest song from the hip-hop group Credible Witness . . ."

Zero was still taking in the news about Zoe when a piercing sound cut through his thoughts and drowned out the Goober broadcast.

The emergency siren, thought Zero.

The warning system in Cégolim sounded different notes depending on the circumstances. Zero knew of twelve different tones. Four were to help organize life in the settlement (mealtimes, the start and end of the workday, Jude's birthday), four were to announce imminent threats (sandstorms, thunderstorms, tornadoes, locusts). He'd forgotten a few of the rest, but he knew this one. He had heard it only once before.

It was the one announcing that an adult had entered the City of Children.

CHAPTER 4

IT wasn't hard to find the intruder. Zero followed the murmur of excited voices like bread crumbs.

The trail led him to the Dragon Pub near the town entrance.

When the adults disappeared, the Dragon Pub was one of the first places the children came to patronize. They were eager to find out what was so special about this place they had been barred from entering. So the children stayed up late and helped themselves to the liquor and beer the adults had forbidden them from drinking. The fun lasted a whole day, but the next day children could be found all around town in advanced stages of miserable drunkenness. Ever since then, everyone stayed well clear of the pub.

A narrow band of children was gathered outside the entrance to the pub.

As Zero got closer, the chatter of voices turned into snatches of conversation.

I heard he's a Saba!

What's that?

A type of security guard, I suppose . . .

I heard he took Jasper prisoner . . .

I hope he doesn't shoot him. He owes me money . . .

The emergency siren went off a second time.

Down the street there came some commotion as Jude, the mayor of the city, arrived. He was seated on a worn mattress resting on wooden planks that were held aloft by four young boys shaking under the collective weight of Jude and his throne. Jude wore black shades and a necklace made of Doran lizard bones, and looked as if someone were holding a cup of something foul under his nose. In his left hand was a scepter—a bamboo stick tied to a large black crystal, which one of the boys had found at one of the digging sites. In Jude's right hand he held Scribbler, a notepad he used to write down the names of people who would have to show up at Fools' Yard the next day. Part of the reason the procession took so much time to arrive was that Jude kept stopping in order to scribble down names—porters who shook the throne a bit too much, or citizens who were wearing colors he didn't like.

Jude's younger brother Jideka walked beside the throne. He was a taller, skinnier version of Jude, with bulging eyes that made him look like he was constantly being strangled. His main contribution to society was to giggle at anything his brother said.

Ahead of the procession were Jude's pet hyenas, Samson and Delilah.

There was a burst of anxious voices. The crowd at the Dragon Pub parted to give a wide birth to the procession—and the hyenas. But as the boys carrying the throne walked up the steps to the pub, they stumbled, and the crowd watched shell-shocked as the bed tipped forward and Jude shot headfirst out of the throne, toppling onto the porch like a split bag of rice. There was a moment of terrified silence.

Jude sat up straight and raised his sunglasses onto his forehead to better see the culprits. He then began furiously scribbling into his notepad the remaining names of his porters, mumbling darkly. He lashed at them with his scepter when they tried to pick him up.

Jude was helped to his feet by Jideka, and together they swept inside the Dragon Pub.

Zero, arm bandaged to disguise the Kobasticker, shouldered his way through the crowd and slipped inside the building.

Inside the Dragon Pub, a tall creature wearing a black suit, black gloves, and a wide-brimmed black hat stood at the bar. He had the face of a lynx, with eyes that glittered with secret knowledge. He was humming a tune and making a show of checking his claws.

Beside the lynx-man was a little boy. His eyes were bright with fear and moved in tight lines from his captor to Jude and back.

"What do you want, stranger? And why are you holding one of my citizens hostage?" said Jude.

The creature smiled, exposing a set of sharp teeth. Behind Zero there was a lot of nervous shuffling.

"My name is Lenoir. I am a Saba who specializes in recovering lost or stolen artifacts. I am currently on the hunt for a dangerous individual named Wanderblatch."

Lenoir reached for something in his pocket. He fished out a silver sphere and let it drop to the floor. The children watched as the ball rolled to a rest. There was a whirring sound, and a beam of blue light shot out of it, displaying a face.

Zero immediately recognized the beast he had seen in the Temple of Ifanabe. It had the same shaggy fur and snout-like nose with the two canines jutting out from under his bottom lip. Wanderblatch turned around, posing from different angles while holding up a placard. Then the beast began to make faces at the camera.

The children flinched. They had never seen holograms like this before.

"I have been tailing this criminal for months now. I have reason to believe he is hiding inside the Temple of Ifanabe. He has in his possession an object I am looking for ..."

Lenoir snapped his fingers and the image on the hologram shifted to show a black-and-gold pyramid. Zero felt something melt inside his stomach—it was the pyramid he had touched. Instinctively, he swung his right arm behind his back.

Lenoir glanced at him sharply.

"This pyramid contains an important Kobasticker," he said, eyes pinning Zero in place.

"I have yet to see how we can help you," said Jude, coldly.

Lenoir's gaze finally cut away from Zero and fell on Jude.

"There are booby traps in the temple. I would need a guide who is familiar with the building. I was thinking I might find someone here."

"So you are taking a hostage?" sneered Jude.

"A bargaining chip. I was not sure what sort of reception I would get here."

"Why should we help you?"

Lenoir shrugged. "The bounty on this man and the object he possesses is quite substantial, more money than I would know what to do with, if I'm being honest. Were you to shelter me until it is safe for me to take to the skies, I would be willing to share some of the bounty. Call it my payment for bed and breakfast."

"What's his bounty?" said Jude.

"Thirty million berries."

Zero gasped. One of the children behind him fainted.

Jude swallowed.

Lenoir smiled. He brushed off an imaginary speck of dust from his shoulder with a clawed finger.

"As I was saying, I would need a guide. Someone who can take me safely into the temple."

Every single head in the room turned toward Zero.

"Is this who I need to see?" asked Lenoir.

"Yes," replied Jude, his eyes letting out sparks.

Zero knew that Jude would rather have put his head between two loaves of bread and into one of his pet hyenas' mouths than have to depend on him. But the realization of how much money he would make seemed to outweigh even his monumental dislike of Zero.

"And why do I have to show him around the temple?" grumbled Zero.

"Because if you don't, you'll be banished from Cégolim," Jude snapped back.

The room fell silent.

Banishings were rare in the city. Zero had only ever heard of two instances. The first had been a boy called Aku, who had killed another boy during a fight. The second had been a girl, Efua. She was older than Zero and he had admired her a lot, but she was constantly butting heads with Jude. She was the daughter of the previous mayor, and most people felt she had a stronger claim to the position, as Jude was only his nephew. But Jude claimed she was a witch and ran her out of town. Most of the children agreed that banishings should only be used in the most extreme of cases.

"You're joking," said Zero.

"Look in my eyes and tell me if I'm joking," Jude snarled. "You flout my authority every chance you get. You don't take part in city activities, and you steal equipment and food from the city stores. Nobody likes you. Even your own mother didn't. If she did, she wouldn't have abandoned you here," he added, with a cruel smile.

Zero felt anger flare inside him like a spray of magma. His whole frame began to shake with Jude's insult. Calming himself took every fiber of control in his body.

Jude used Zero's mother as a weapon to cut away at Zero's pride and heart in a way that his authority and his power never could.

"I could banish you today and not one person here would bat an eyelid."

Zero looked around the room. All the children were avoiding his gaze, and for the first time in his life he saw that what Jude said was true. The realization hit him like a punch to the gut.

"When would you like to go?" Zero asked Lenoir, his voice trembling with emotion.

"This evening. Nine o'clock."

Zero nodded. *Nine o'clock*. The words seemed detached from all meaning. His head was still ringing from Jude's insult.

Jude, Lenoir, and some of Jude's underlings headed off on a tour of the city, and Zero—humiliated and distraught—rushed home, feeling the eyes of the rest of the children on him.

Zero had just settled in for a measly dinner when the intruder siren rang a second time, and he made his way back to the Dragon Pub. A pair of men in black robes and wide-brimmed hats had arrived to meet with Jude. They were from a boutique bounty-hunting firm called Faaris & Faaris. When they caught sight of Lenoir sitting alone at a table in a corner of the pub, waiting for a room to be ready for him, they quickly walked over and introduced themselves. They seemed eager to be on his good side.

The tranquillity of the City of Children was disturbed once again when barely ten minutes later the intruder siren rang once more. This time, three brothers arrived dressed in black ponchos and cowboy boots. They approached Jude and introduced themselves as members of a prestigious family of bounty hunters. They greeted the two recently arrived men, but when they saw Lenoir they did a double take. They took off their hats and quickly went over to greet him. Lenoir listened politely to what they had to say, like a monarch meeting subjects.

A steady stream of strangers arrived in the city over the course of the afternoon.

Before long the intruder alarm began to sound with increasing frequency, as if announcing a planetary invasion.

Afterward, Zero would see the boy who manned the town's siren mechanism cradling his hand in obvious discomfort.

With each ring, a new group of adults arrived in the town. They met Jude in the center square, where they introduced themselves and handed him their business cards. They came from agencies such as One Shot and Bounties Without Borders, and they wore everything from sharp suits to bright-colored kaftans.

A small army had begun to form around the Dragon Pub, and as their ranks increased they became rowdy. Jude seemed powerless to quiet them down. In fact, the ruler of Cégolim seemed to have slowly relinquished his authority with each consecutive wave of strangers. He began to avoid the Dragon Pub altogether.

Zero of course had no sympathy to spare for him.

Zero noticed that the new arrivals seemed to hold Lenoir in high regard. They fell silent whenever they got near, and they all went over to greet him. No one dared to join him where he sat reading a newspaper.

Zero began to worry about Wanderblatch. He knew that he had to alert him somehow but found himself constantly in demand by the strangers, who needed food, mechanical parts, or information about the Temple of Ifanabe.

By the time he was finally able to sneak away for a moment to breathe, the light had leached out of the sky and the twin moons of Anansi 12 had emerged.

He was walking between two clay huts when he heard two voices ahead. Their conversation made him freeze.

"Why are we letting cat guy take the lead? Why don't we just go to the temple without him?" asked the first voice.

"You must not be very bright. Four bounty hunters had the very same idea and tried to sneak out to the temple earlier today. They didn't get very far before Lenoir caught up to them," answered the second voice.

"Why don't we just take it off him once he's got it? With all the bounty hunters here, we could overpower him!"

"Take it off him? Have you lost your mind, you fool?" hissed the second voice. "Don't you know who he is? That's Billion-Berrie Lenoir. He's the best bounty hunter there is. You want to have a Kobasticker found or retrieved? He's your guy. They say that Lenoir's made over a billion berries in reward money over the years."

There was an appreciative whistle before the second voice continued speaking.

"I heard he was employed by a secret cult of space wizards who believe that the Kobasticker threatens their existence."

"I still don't understand what's so special about a Kobasticker," grumbled the first voice unhappily.

"It's one of the most sought-after Kobastickers in the whole galaxy. It's one from the Origin series, and it's meant to hold the key to immortality. If you believe the rumors, every thirteenth wielder of the Kobasticker is gifted with immortality. The last user of the Kobasticker was the twenty-fourth user, so I don't know why anyone would want to inherit it next. They would likely be the most hunted man in the galaxy. It would be like having a huge bull's-eye on your back. Not to mention, anyone still loyal to Zomon the Dark King is going to be looking for you. Together with the Zodiac Sabas, the Origin Sabas fought to defeat Zomon and seal him off. You can bet your last berry that Zomon hasn't forgotten that. If he ever returns, he is going to be coming for every last one of those Kobastickers to make sure no one ever stands up to him again."

The voice paused, and a chill passed through Zero at the ominous words. Instinctively, he clutched his bandaged arm.

"At any rate, I wouldn't want to be in Wanderblatch's shoes. Lenoir is known for never leaving any loose ends. He'll be murdered, if he's lucky."

At this, the two voices broke into a loud guffaw.

Zero had heard enough. He was backing away, his heart in his throat, when he bumped into someone.

"Oy, look where you're going, you dimwit!" cried a voice.

Zero looked up.

The two bounty hunters who had arrived immediately after Lenoir were glaring down at him.

"Lenoir wants to see you, boy. He says that you are to accompany him to the temple right now, so step to it quick!" growled the one to the left, who was massaging the spot on his stomach where Zero had bumped into him.

His stomach churning with anxiety, Zero made his way back to the Dragon Pub.

CHAPTER 5

ZERO, Lenoir, Jude, and a procession of bounty hunters set off for the Temple of Ifanabe at nine o'clock. The atmosphere was peculiar.

Lenoir had assembled the group of them around the Tree of Bob. Most of the bounty hunters had not been there when he had struck a deal with Jude and Zero, so Lenoir had explained how he would go into the Temple of Ifanabe and retrieve the pyramid with Zero as his guide. Once he retrieved the pyramid, they would all return to the city with it and as a delegation they would cash the bounty.

The other bounty hunters had been silent for a moment but then began to grumble.

"Why do you get to go alone to find the treasure?" one of the bounty hunters had asked.

"Yeah!" another shouted.

"Either we all go or nobody goes!"

Lenoir, feeling for the first time that he might have overstepped his authority, had backed down. So he, Zero, Jude, and all the rest of the bounty hunters left for the temple together.

Dark clouds stretched across the sky and flared with flashes of silent lightning.

The whole way, Zero kept thinking of ways to weasel out of the situation. He found none.

Any way he looked at it—he was stuck.

If he did what Lenoir said, he would be betraying Wanderblatch. He thought about him stranded in the temple, and shuddered as he imagined the look of disappointment on his face when he realized Zero's betrayal.

If there was anyone else who seemed particularly unhappy with the turn of events, it was Jude. He and his underlings were notably silent as they made their trip through the desert. There were no taunts, and there was no bragging. His face looked troubled in the pale orange glow emanating from the crystal in his scepter.

Lenoir's arrival had upended a lot of things in the city. Zero had noticed it a few times before, but in Lenoir's presence Jude seemed to regress to the child he really was. All the bluster and the posturing were gone.

As they approached the temple, the ground suddenly began to shake.

Zero looked up just in time to see a giant bolt of lightning shoot out from the top of the Adesha's head and fork up to the sky. It was like looking upside down at a giant, incandescent tree root.

There was a boom of thunder, and the bolt of lightning winked out of existence.

The company halted. There was some anxious chatter before Lenoir said, "Do not be afraid. Very soon we will be in possession of what we came for."

As he peered up at the temple, Zero thought it looked more like a skull than a woman's face.

He also knew that he was running out of time. He needed to find a way to be alone with Wanderblatch, to warn him.

It was now or never. Zero cleared his throat.

"Mr. Lenoir?"

His voice sounded raspy and weak.

"What is it, young man?"

"I was thinking ... Going into the temple, finding the object you seek, will be impossible with these numbers. The foundations are shaky, and in some parts the paths and tunnels are incredibly narrow."

"So what do you suggest?" asked Lenoir.

"Why don't I go in and fetch the object for you? I know the temple very well, so it should be a lot quicker for me to find it. You might slow me down. Then I could come back here and give it to you."

Lenoir regarded Zero for a long time in silence. Zero knew that though his argument made sense, it was not enough to convince Lenoir. He would have to present it to the rest of the company, and what's more, convince them. He knew that it would be no easy task. Right now the bounty hunters were all aligned and focused on one objective.

"What's he going on about?" asked one of the bounty hunters.

"This young man has proposed that, as the person among us that knows the temple the best, he alone could find the location of Wanderblatch and the pyramid and bring it to us. I personally think it would be the best thing to do."

The bounty hunters seemed to agree with him. Zero going

was a harmless compromise. He had no stake in finding the pyramid, and so would be less likely to double-cross them, as one of their own number might.

"Now remember, my boy: All you have to do is find Wanderblatch, take the pyramid, and then come right back here. Don't do anything silly, don't try to be a hero."

Zero was about to set off when Lenoir added, "Just a moment."

Lenoir reached out and grabbed Zero by the wrist. He then tore off Zero's bandage, letting it fall like an orange peel onto the desert floor.

The Kobasticker was gone! Or at least, what Zero had thought was a Kobasticker was gone.

"I guess I was imagining things," murmured Lenoir, looking narrowly at Zero. "I also think you should take this." He pulled a small pistol with a golden hilt from his pocket.

At the sight of it, Zero blanched.

"I don't think I'll need this—" he began.

"You never know."

He lobbed it at him but Zero fumbled it, dropping it to the ground.

This made the others jeer and laugh.

Zero put the pistol in his coat pocket with trembling hands and hurried to the entrance to the temple.

Once he was inside, Zero felt relieved. He was finally out of the constricting presence of the others. He made his way through the exhibit hall. The two Goymons were nowhere in sight.

He was wondering how he would tell Wanderblatch

about the situation when his feet struck something lying across his path.

Zero stumbled headfirst onto the ground.

"Sand God, save me!" cried a voice.

"Bo?"

"Zero?"

"What are you doing inside here!"

"I heard there was some commotion from my brothers. They said a lot of strange people had arrived and were headed to the temple. I wanted to be in on the action! I knew that you wouldn't let me join if I asked you, so I came early and waited here."

Zero chewed the inside of his cheek.

He didn't want to take Bo along, but he had very little choice now. "Alright then, follow me and be quiet."

Wanderblatch was slumped against the side of the marble tomb in the same crypt chamber where Zero had first found him. His eyes were closed, his chin rested on his chest, and his hands were dangling limply at his sides. At the sight of him, Bo made a start.

Wanderblatch's eyes flew open and settled on them.

"You came back," he said, smiling. His teeth shone with the sickly pallor of lemon rind. "A friend of yours?"

"This is Bo," Zero explained. "What happened?"

"Nothing you should be worried about," he said. He struggled to his feet with a tremendous groan. "What are you two doing here, at this hour?"

Zero told him everything, about Lenoir and the others who were outside waiting for a signal, and about the theft of the pyramid.

"I'm sorry," said Zero, unable to hold his gaze.

"No need to apologize. You did what you had to do."

Wanderblatch took a deep, rattling breath. "What our friend Lenoir is after is what was contained in that pyramid, which now resides in you."

"In me?" Zero gaped.

Wanderblatch nodded, and Bo looked at him in awe.

"What do you know about Koba?" Wanderblatch continued.

Zero gathered his thoughts.

"I know that it's a form of stardust with magical properties."

Wanderblatch nodded. "Precisely. The first users of Kobastickers were called 'lords of stardust.' The first Kobastickers were created by the Maniki, a race of alien nomads who traveled the universe gathering all the magic, spells, and knowledge they could find and used special technology to turn them into Kobastickers. They then spread their knowledge to the different races and people. Most Kobastickers contain low-level spells—for levitation and heating things, for instance. But some are more powerful than others. These have unique properties that make them extremely sought after by people throughout the galaxy."

Wanderblatch paused. "The pyramid that you touched contained a very rare Kobasticker: Jupiter. It is one of the twenty-four legendary Origin Kobastickers named after the objects in the solar system," he said.

Zero stared at Wanderblatch, realization dawning on him.

"In *me*?" he gasped.

"I think you are finally beginning to understand."

Wanderblatch shifted on the floor, grunting painfully. "The Jupiter chose you, Zero. I never would have expected to find a successor to Jupiter in such a distant part of the galaxy—and a human child at that. It is a cruel fate: possessing the Jupiter means one is hunted constantly, by criminals looking to make money or by Sabas looking to obtain the secrets of immortality. Your faith in others will be tested. You will see the worst in people. You will experience violence. But in all this you must not lose faith in humanity. I cannot question the Jupiter's will. As its guardian, I can only keep it safe until it finds a worthy new heir."

By now, a few curious Goymons had crept into the chamber and were standing a little ways away from Zero, Bo, and Wanderblatch.

"Listen to me, Zero. Lenoir is a very dangerous man. In my current state, I am no match for him, but together we might have a chance. He must not know that Jupiter has passed on to you. I have the pyramid, and if he comes we will let him take it."

"But if the Kobasticker is no longer in the pyramid, the pyramid will be worthless!"

"Yes, but he doesn't know that."

A mix of admiration and fear fizzed in Zero's stomach. "So we can just give it to him, and he won't realize it is empty! Where is the briefcase?" he asked.

Wanderblatch pulled out the cone-shaped briefcase from behind the tomb and opened it, holding out the pyramid.

Zero hesitated before reaching for the pyramid. The last time he had touched it, he had been blasted off his feet. This time, there wasn't so much as a spark when he took it in his hands.

Zero felt the weight of this important task. Someone was coming here to do Wanderblatch harm, and he had to defend him.

"Good. But from this point on, no matter what he does, we must not let him know about the pyramid."

"Know what?"

Zero wheeled around. Bo let out a shout of alarm.

Lenoir was standing in the entrance to the chamber, his hands behind his back and a wicked grin on his face. Behind him stood Jude and a narrow band of bounty hunters.

"What is it about that pyramid I should know, gentlemen?"

But before Wanderblatch could speak, Lenoir shouted, "*Koba-Blackflash!*"

A Kobasticker that looked like a hand with a black thunderbolt diagonally across it appeared in a shower of sparks in front of Lenoir. He plucked it out of the air and placed it on his forearm all in under a second.

He aimed a bolt of black light from a gloved finger at Wanderblatch's shoulder. Wanderblatch spun like a top and crumpled to the floor in a heap.

"Wanderblatch!" screamed Zero, rushing to his side.

"This is a favorite of mine. All the other Kobastickers in the Flash series are jokes compared to this one. Perfect for duels. It fires an energy blast that stuns the victim with unimaginable pain, which, in my line of work, is always a plus."

Lenoir approached them slowly, his eyes trained on Wanderblatch. "That was a nice trick you pulled on us near the Lotox asteroid belt. I don't know how you managed to survive that explosion, but it doesn't matter now."

"Why are you here?" rasped Wanderblatch, rising on unsteady feet.

"A client of mine happens to have his eyes on the Kobasticker contained in that pyramid of yours . He's part of a group that calls itself the Cult of the Six-Star Vessel. They believe that the birth of a twenty-sixth user of the Jupiter will doom their order. A loony bunch of cuckoos, if you ask me, but their money is very real."

"I don't understand. With all your power, you still end up working as a lapdog for some mad cult?"

Lenoir made a show of inspecting his nails.

"It pays the bills. You should try it. It beats being murdered in an ancient temple in the middle of nowhere, that's for sure," he said meaningfully.

He walked over to Zero's side. "You did well, Zero."

Zero tried to open his mouth to speak, but his voice would not work.

"I tailed you," Lenoir explained. "I know we had an agreement, but the boys were growing restless, you see. Luckily, the pistol I gave you contains a small tracker, so we were able to find you. Now hand me the pyramid, Zero," he said coldly.

"Don't!" cried Bo.

Zero looked at Wanderblatch. For a split second their gazes held and Wanderblatch give him a slight nod.

"Hand it over," replied Lenoir, slowly. "I could kill you for it right now, but I would rather we do this the civilized way."

Zero gave one last glance at Wanderblatch, then handed over the pyramid to Lenoir.

A grin broke out across his lynx face until his expression was pure evil delight.

"You have what you want. Now let him go," said Wanderblatch.

Lenoir seemed to consider this.

"I suppose you are right. Some type of reward is in order. *Blackflash*," said Lenoir. The Kobasticker on his forearm began to glow, and before Zero could react, two successive black rays struck Wanderblatch in the gut.

Wanderblatch stumbled backward, clutching his stomach. His eyes wide in shock, he gasped for breath like a fish out of water. He collapsed like a felled tree.

Zero cried out, bending down to try to help him.

Lenoir turned and faced the bounty hunters, proudly brandishing the pyramid.

"We've got what we came for, boys," he said smugly.

No one moved. The bounty hunters stared past the three of them with a strange expression on their faces. It almost looked like terror.

"What's the matter?" asked Lenoir.

One of the bounty hunters raised a trembling hand and pointed at something behind them.

Lenoir turned around as a shadow swept over him.

Zero looked up to find Fido looming over them. He had emerged from the open crypt and was standing with his front paws on the lip of the tomb, ropes of saliva stretching from his razor teeth. He let out a menacing growl.

Zero and Bo ducked as Fido went sailing over them and pounced on Lenoir. Fido fastened his teeth around Lenoir's torso and shook his head violently, throwing the bounty hunter around like a rag doll before dragging him screaming into the crypt.

The bounty hunters scattered, like beads from a torn necklace. Zero and Bo hooked their hands under Wanderblatch's armpits to drag him away from the crypt and the chilling gnashing noises that came from within it. There was a black flash, and a yelp of agony as Fido shot out of the tomb and fell heavily on the hard floor. Zero smelled singed fur and burning flesh as Fido rolled on the ground, desperately trying to put out little bursts of black flames on his belly.

Zero looked toward the opening of the crypt just as Lenoir emerged, a crazed look on his face, the fur on his neck matted with blood.

"Nice try. Where is the Jupiter?" he demanded in a voice like the blade of a dagger. He held up the pyramid in his hand, and Zero saw with a shock that it was torn open, like the remains of a fruit. It was clear to see that it was empty.

"Jupiter! Where is it!" he roared, his voice thick with rage.

"You're much too late," Wanderblatch rasped. "The Jupiter has already chosen its next host."

Realization dawned on Lenoir and he turned to look at Zero, hunger glinting in his eyes.

"You," he breathed.

"You're too late," Wanderblatch said again. "The lightning you saw on your way to the temple? It was me sending out a message. They will be here any moment now." He coughed, a gush of blood spilling down his chin.

Lenoir's gaze cut to Wanderblatch. His eyes were like openings into a burning furnace.

"You're bluffing," he spat.

"We will find out pretty soon, won't we? A Saba guild. One of the best."

Lenoir swore.

"Ah, but you see there is still such a thing as professional pride. If I can't have the Kobasticker, I can at least bring back your body," he said, rounding on Zero. The Kobasticker on his arm began to glow once more. "Nothing personal, kid. I'm just having a very bad day at work."

Panic was a hot iron in Zero's chest as Lenoir strode toward him, his face mottled with fury. "For what it's worth, that was a nice try with that dog, but you would need a lot more to get rid of me," Lenoir growled.

"We're counting on it," said Wanderblatch.

Lenoir laughed sardonically. "Please don't tell me you expect something else to come crawling out of that crypt to save you." He raised his arm, a Kobasticker already forming on his skin.

"No, not from the tomb," replied Wanderblatch, looking up toward the ceiling.

"What nonsense are you spout—"

The room erupted into chaos.

There was a deafening roar, and the room was flooded with light as something burst through the ceiling. It struck the platform with such force that the ground under Zero's feet seemed to undulate. He was blasted with a wall of dust and stone fragments and collapsed, his skull smacking the floor. He tried to breathe but broke out coughing.

Zero fought to stay conscious as he heard two voices bickering.

"Ladi?"

"Yes, Camih?"

"I'm going to go out on a limb and suggest this might be your fourth-worst landing of all time."

"Not my best work, I grant you that, but did you see the asteroid belt I had to navigate through?"

There was a short silence after which the first voice said:

"Ladi?"

"Yes, Camih?"

"I think you might have landed on someone."

There was a groan.

"I think that makes it the third worst."

Through a cloud of dust, a figure emerged. It was tall and had its hands on its hips in a familiar posture.

"*Zoe* . . ." said Zero faintly.

But his consciousness narrowed into a dot. Then that dot blinked out.

CHAPTER 6

ZERO fell into a state between wakefulness and sleep. His body was on fire and there was a searing pain in his head that rose inexorably in intensity like the mercury on a thermometer.

At one time Zero had the impression that a figure was crouched beside him. He felt something brush against his lips, and then a delicious numbness spread through his body.

Zero slipped into a strange dream of a scene from his past. Zero was curled in a corner of a dark chamber, his head on his knees and his arms wrapped around his shins.

There was the sound of footsteps, and when he looked up, Zoe was standing over him.

"What is going on, Zero? Why have you been avoiding me lately?"

"You're leaving and I don't want you to go," he said, looking at the ground. "People I love end up leaving me here all alone. It's happening again. I don't want to be alone again. It's not fair." Zero's eyes began to burn with tears.

Zoe crouched down and looked at him full on.

"I'm sorry, Zero. But Kadj and I can't stay here forever. You know that. Now that our whizzer is repaired, we have to continue our voyage and finish our mission. The Space Force is after us."

Zero nodded, but he felt stupid. He'd planned for this to be a simple and mature discussion, but losing Zoe had knocked him back into the crying, temperamental child he used to be.

"How is your Ewodo progressing?" she asked gently. "Are you able to read the hieroglyphs on the third floor yet?"

Zero said that he could, and she straightened up.

"Time for a little magic trick."

She pressed her hands together, and as she pulled them apart a vinyl record in a red paper sleeve dropped to the floor.

"No way!" cried Zero.

"An R5 album. My favorite Afrobeats group. Their latest album, *Andromeda 2000*, wasn't very good, but this is their classic, *Milky Way*. I hope it will bring you just as much pleasure as it did me."

Zero held it tightly to his chest, and Zoe grinned.

"Don't move!" she gasped. "I think I see something behind your ear."

Zero smiled as she reached behind his ear and brought out a beautiful gold medallion.

Zero's eyes grew to the size of plates as she placed the medallion in his hand. It was shaped like an orb connected to a comb.

"This shows that we are family. And if you ever need me, you can present this to anyone who knows me and they will owe you a favor. I used to be like you, Zero. I came from a small planet in the middle of nowhere. But I know someday you will become an extraordinary Saba, better than Kadj or I will ever be. Do you hear me?"

She hugged Zero tightly. She smelled warm, like honey and sunsets and the glow from a campfire.

When she pulled back, Zero wiped his tears with the back of his hand.

Slowly, she undid her kente bandanna and tied it around his neck.

Zoe raised his chin gently with a finger.

"You are going to be all right, Zero. That I promise you. Start up your rescue business. I'm sure it will be incredibly successful. We will see each other soon. And if you are ever in trouble and need my help, write to me on Sigmia and I will drop down here in no time. Deal?"

Zero nodded.

The scene faded as Zero felt himself waking up.

When Zero opened his eyes, Bo was kneeling beside him, glaring at him.

"Am I in Nagoni?" Zero said. Surely he was in the sacred hall where the souls of worthy Sabas gathered after they passed away.

"I don't think so. We're in Jude's house."

Zero wrinkled his nose.

"What's that smell?"

"Some Komodo cheese I got from home. Would you like some?"

Bo fumbled inside his knapsack next to him and pulled out something pale and soggy wrapped in dried plantain leaves. The smell rose up and clobbered Zero across the face. And he'd thought that Dralaxian cheese smelled bad.

He nearly gagged.

"No thanks," he said, pinching his nostrils shut.

"Suit yourself."

Zero sat up slowly. "Why are you looking at me like that? You look like I stole something from you."

"I'm jealous!"

"Because I almost died? You're welcome to take my place."

"Not because of that!" He looked toward the open door, which told Zero that someone was outside, and dropped his voice to a whisper.

"You were knocked unconscious by the blast, but the lady said you had been courageous and she . . . she kissed you on the cheek!"

Zero felt blood rush to his face.

"Well, I was too busy fighting for my life to remember it.," he groaned, trying to sit up.

"The lady told me to come and see if you were feeling better. I think they want to speak with us," said Bo.

Zero looked at the door to the hall. It was incredible how passing through that simple opening now seemed daunting.

The two visitors were sitting at a rough-hewn table.

The boy was bent over a glowing square-shaped Kobasticker. He was handsome in an effortless kind of way, with violet hair, matching eyebrows, a hard jaw, and deep-set eyes. Several welding tools were floating around his head. The boy had a magnifying glass on his eye and plucked tools out of the air as he repaired the Kobasticker. Orange sparks sprayed from the corner of the Kobasticker, lighting his face in a soft glow. He wiped his sweaty brow as the girl spoke to him.

"How are things advancing?" asked the girl.

"Not very well. If I don't repair this Kobasticker soon, we won't be able to go home."

The girl nodded. She looked up and beamed at the sight of Zero.

"Hey you! Feeling better?" She rose from her seat. "I'm Camih Sitso."

Zero felt something wobble inside his chest as he looked at Zoe's sister.

She had deep, curious eyes that shone like sunlight winking through palm fronds. Her hair was styled in long dreadlocks, and a smile seemed to permanently hover at the corner of her lips.

She did look a lot like Zoe. She was tall and pretty, but not the way a new whizzer or a diamond ring is beautiful. Zoe was beautiful in the dignified way of old temples and ancient monuments.

"So great of you to join us. We were scared you wouldn't make it. At least he was." She nodded to the boy. "This is Ladi—"

"Hyung," finished Zero. "I've heard about you. You're both Sabas from the Shango Heart Guild."

Camih and Ladi looked at each other.

"Camih Sitso. You've got two million followers on Sigmia—"

"Two million one hundred thousand, but who's counting?" she interrupted smugly.

"You made the list of the Top Twenty-Five Sabas to Watch and won the Saba Association's Under Thirty Best Duelists competition two years running. You finished third in *Zebra* magazine's Most Beautiful Sabas in the Galaxy list," continued Zero.

"They're just accolades. I never pay too much attention to them!" Camih replied, waving away Zero's compliments.

"But you have also been involved in a few scandals. You rammed your whizzer into the space shuttle of a journalist who was publishing critical articles about you."

"That case is still in the courts, so I can't really—"

"You attacked a convoy that was carrying food for troll refugees on the planet Okorie 13."

"My intel told me they were smuggling defective Kobastickers—"

"And that's not all—"

"Okay, that's enough!" shouted Camih. "I've made some mistakes in my life, I get it! And you obviously have been keeping score!"

"I think I'm going to like this guy," said Ladi, grinning.

Camih glared at him.

Zero turned to look at Ladi.

"And you—" began Zero.

Ladi jumped up and latched his hands around Zero's mouth.

"Don't you start with me! I'm a nobody!" he cried.

Zero shrugged.

"Have a seat, Zero," said Camih, pointing to a chair beside her at the end of the table.

Zero walked over and sat down.

"What happened? Back in the temple?" asked Zero.

"Well, it seems we saved you from a tough spot, bud. Lenoir was about to kill you," said Ladi.

"Where is he?"

Ladi shrugged. "We don't know. He must have found a way to escape Anansi 12. At any rate, he's going to be out of commission for a while."

"What about Jude? And the bounty hunters?"

"The leader of your city ran away into the desert, and the others fled. Most of them hit booby traps in their hurry to escape the guardian of the temple."

"What about Wanderblatch?"

Camih and Ladi stared at each other.

Zero described what had happened to Wanderblatch. When he was done, Ladi snapped his fingers, as if remembering something.

"A Nimba Guardian!"

"A what now?" asked Zero.

"A Nimba Guardian. Certain rare and powerful Kobastickers have them. A spirit in charge of protecting the Kobastickers and ensuring they are passed on to the right people. I hear they act as advisers or companions sometimes. At least that is what we read about in Kobasticker history class, isn't that right, Camih?"

"Sounds about right," said Camih.

"I see. What about Fido?" asked Zero.

Almost in answer, there came a booming bark from outside the window. Fido's great big face appeared by the window, darkening the room.

"He's doing fine. We brought him here and healed him. He's been a hit with the other children here."

Camih shifted, her expression turning serious. "Zero,

there is something we need to talk to you about. It concerns the Jupiter."

She leaned in so close to him he could smell her perfume. It made him think of gold dust and sunsets and the interior of luxury spaceships.

"Zero, how would you like to join Shango Heart?" asked Camih.

If Zero hadn't been sitting, he might have collapsed.

Bo let out a shriek.

"M-me, become a Saba?" gasped Zero.

"That is certainly the plan. We would take you to our guild, where you can learn how to use your newfound Kobasticker," said Camih, and began to recite: "*By decree of the Children of Stardust Act, any child who, by the age of thirteen, has been chosen by Koba and has bonded with a Class B or higher Kobasticker, must be recruited to a Saba guild so that they may learn to harness it.* There hasn't been a child of stardust in this part of the galaxy for a few years."

She glanced at Ladi. "And then there is another reason . . ."

"Due to the very nature of the Kobasticker you have, we can't leave you here. It's only a matter of time before even more Kobasticker hunters, bounty hunters, and all manner of dangerous criminals show up and try to do you in, bud," said Ladi.

"Have you heard of the space witches' prophecy about Jupiter?" asked Camih.

"That every thirteenth user of the Jupiter is granted immortality," replied Zero, nodding.

"That's right. You're the twenty-fifth, so we're going

to have to teach you to defend yourself and become a competent Saba."

Zero's head was spinning.

"I'll need some time to think," he said. His mind felt like a crowded blazeball stadium when a team has just scored a goal.

"Take the night. Think it through," Camih said softly. "But we leave for the guild headquarters first thing tomorrow morning."

"I understand."

"One last thing."

"Yes?"

"Don't overthink things." She grinned widely. "That was an emergency medical procedure, not a kiss."

CHAPTER 7

THAT night Zero lay on his bed wide awake. He thought about Camih's purported medical kiss and felt heat rise to his face, but he also couldn't believe he was going to become a Sabin: a Saba student.

He decided to write Zoe an email to inform her that he was joining a Saba guild, and not just any guild: the one she had learned her craft from. And Jupiter was a lightning type Kobasticker, just like hers. She owned the legendary Sagittarius Zodiac Kobasticker, which allowed her to control the weather. That's how she got the nickname Stormfox. He opened his Goober (he had to plug his right nostril with a piece of cloth after the Goober plucked a nose hair too hard) and began to write his message. When he was done, he hesitated with his finger hovering over the Send button. He wondered if his latest email would get added to the long list of unanswered messages he had already sent her. He sent it anyway.

Ten minutes later, he was fast asleep.

When he woke up the next morning, he was a ball of excitement. He was going to be joining a famous Saba guild!

Zero thought of his mother. He had always told himself that if he were able to build a name for himself and climb the Saba ranks, then the stories of his deeds would spread across the galaxy. And if he became famous enough, then his mother would hear of him, and she would remember the boy she had left behind and maybe—just maybe—she would want to take him back.

Zero took one last look at his room, at the posters and the objects on the stone shelves that he had accumulated from years of rescuing space travelers in the desert. The place seemed to belong to someone else. Someone who was chasing a dream that was impossible. And he was no longer that person. He did his best to imprint all the details of his room on the film of his memory. Then he got ready to find Camih and Ladi.

A small procession of children had gathered in the main square. Many were busy ogling Fido, who was rolling around in the sun.

Camih and Ladi were already there.

"Glad you could make it," said Camih.

The early morning sun lit the contours of her face. She seemed to be glowing.

"Are you ready? We can give you a moment to say your final goodbyes," said Camih.

He turned to have a good look at the faces that made a circle around him. He noticed Bo, who was shedding enough tears to water a forest.

Judika was standing at the front of the group. He had Jude's scepter in his hand, but some of the older children were holding his arms as if he were a prisoner. He looked bruised and crestfallen. Jude hadn't returned from the desert, and now Judika was the only remaining symbol of the old regime. The children tugged him forward and he approached Zero, not looking him in the eye.

"Become our leader, Zero," he mumbled.

Zero gaped, looking at the surrounding faces.

"But I won't be here! I don't know when—" he began.

"It doesn't matter!" Judika interrupted. "They—I mean, *we* have decided we want you to be our leader! Please," he added quickly when one of the children pinched him. He held out the scepter to Zero.

It had been so integral to Jude that it looked alien and strange without him. An ordinary bamboo stick with a crystal tied to one end.

Zero took it, feeling a burn of emotion in the back of his throat.

"I thank you for the honor. My first gesture as mayor will be to ask you all for a favor. This is my friend Bo," he said, reaching out and wrapping his arm around Bo. "He is a Desert Bunny but he is also a dear friend of mine. He will stand in for me as mayor until I return."

There were gasps and some chattering, but no one complained. Bo looked up at Zero, his eyes wide and full of tears.

Zero handed the scepter to Bo, who held it with hands that trembled so much Zero was afraid he would drop it.

Zero turned to look at Camih.

"I'm ready."

Camih nodded and said, "*Koba-Ladybug.*"

With a tiny thunderclap, a Kobasticker materialized in midair. It was the Kobasticker Zero had seen Ladi repairing in Jude's quarters.

Camih plucked it out of the air and placed it on her forearm. She aimed a beam of yellow light at a patch of laterite soil in front of her.

There was a flash of light, and a spaceship bubbled into shape.

The children gasped. They had never seen space magic like that before.

It was Camih's whizzer, the *Ladybug*, which had crashed inside the Temple of Ifanabe. Only it didn't look like a ladybug right now. It looked more like it had been placed in the path of a stampede of giant desert bison. The front was bashed in and one of the wings hung lower than the other. But the red-and-black ladybug pattern remained.

"Don't mind the aesthetics, bud. It may look in bad shape, but it will get us safely back to the guild," said Ladi.

Zero cast a final look around the square. A wave of sadness swirled inside him. He felt a sharp pain in the back of his throat, and his eyes prickled with emotion.

"Let's go," he said.

Ladi wrapped his arm around Zero's shoulders, and together they climbed into the whizzer.

CHAPTER 8

SHANGO Heart Guild was located in the Dorkenoo asteroid belt. It was a tall manor perched on a large asteroid the shape of a baked potato. The glass windows had louvered exterior blinds, and a balcony jutted from the top floor. A giant flashing neon sign that read "Shango Heart Guild" floated above the manor, basking the asteroid in a pale pink light. The top right-hand corner of the sign let off sparks of light.

"Welcome to Shango Heart, Zero," said Camih.

As the whizzer approached, Zero stared in awe at the building. The glow from the nearest star sent sweeping shafts of pale blue light across the asteroid's atmosphere, making it look like the guild was floating on a sea of blue smoke.

The shadow of a small stray asteroid glided over the *Ladybug*, heading toward the manor. Zero watched as it struck an invisible barrier and exploded into a thousand tiny fragments that fell on either side of their whizzer.

"A protective barrier against asteroids and space debris," Camih explained. "It is a common thing. The manor used to be the prestigious Langley Hotel. The first guildmaster bought it after it fell into disrepair, and it's been Shango Heart ever since."

The *Ladybug* was on its last legs as it approached the manor. It puffed ominous smoke, and there were rattling sounds coming from the engine. Staring out of the cockpit,

Zero gasped as he saw a few plates from the hood of the whizzer pop out and fly into space.

Ladi swallowed audibly.

The *Ladybug* made its way toward the base of the asteroid, where a giant hidden door opened like a shutter on a camera lens at their approach. A beam of white light shot out from deep inside the opening and engulfed the whizzer. Zero felt a sharp tug as the ship was jerked forward toward the opening.

"A net-beam," said Camih by way of explanation.

They entered a hangar lit by giant electric ceiling lamps. Hundreds of whizzers were stationed at docks positioned up and down a central cylinder that dropped from the roof like a stalk of metallic bananas. Around the docks hurried strange creatures Zero had never seen before.

"What are those creatures?" asked Zero.

"Geekaloos," replied Camih.

They looked like monkeys but with white fur and blue hands and feet. All wore aviator helmets and either a red vest or a gray jumpsuit. They held repair tools and were jumping up and down, chattering excitedly.

Ladi edged the whizzer closer to Landing Dock 8. One hundred feet . . . fifty feet . . . When it was about ten feet away, the *Ladybug* gave a final, terrible gargle and fell out of the sky.

Zero shut his eyes and gritted his teeth, preparing for the plunge.

But momentum carried the ship forward just enough. The Geekaloos around Dock 8 bolted as the *Ladybug* slammed into the dock, emitting a cloud of black smoke.

When the three finally emerged from the hatch at the back of the whizzer, they were submerged in the welcoming committee of Geekaloos standing on the passerelle.

A tall android dressed in a blue tuxedo with cloud motifs and a yellow bow tie stood behind the furry creatures. It had a silver head, a black glass strip as a visor, and two silver doorknobs for ears.

"So glad to see you back, madam," it greeted Camih. "I trust your travels have been successful?"

"They have, thank you, Anton."

"I take it you will need the Geekaloos to have a look at your spaceship, madam," Anton said, nodding toward the smoking whizzer.

"I would very much need that, thank you, Anton."

The android nodded. He clapped two times, and the Geekaloos rushed toward the whizzer.

Camih turned to Zero. "Zero, this is Anton, the guild's android butler. Anton, this is Zero Adedji, an unregistered Saba candidate. He will be looking to join our guild."

Zero smiled at the android, and Anton nodded again.

"Ah yes, madam. He will be looking to see Mr. Gauche then."

"Yes, Anton. Is he around?"

"He is currently entertaining members of the Compliance Committee from the Intergalactic Saba Organization."

"That doesn't sound good," Ladi muttered.

"Who are they?" asked Zero.

"The Compliance Committee is in charge of guild licenses," said Camih.

"They hate us," added Ladi.

All of a sudden there was an earsplitting explosion behind them.

They all whirled around to see the *Ladybug* burst into flames. Plumes of black smoke curled upward toward the roof.

"Aw, man, that is not good," groaned Ladi.

The carcass of the whizzer gave a tremendous sigh as it collapsed in on itself.

Geekaloos began forming a water line and were hurling buckets of water at it.

Anton herded the crew away from the wreckage and through a corridor. Antique chandeliers threw arrows of light on the black curlicue wallpaper, and long red carpets lined the corridors.

"What have I missed?" Camih asked Anton.

"Nothing much, my lady. You have letters from *Saba Lady* magazine asking for an interview for a piece on up-and-coming female Sabas breaking boundaries," said Anton.

"What about me, Anton?" Ladi interjected. "Surely I must have a few interview requests too. Maybe *Saba Now* finally wants to have me on their Young Sabas to Watch list." He winked at Zero.

"We did get some mail for you, sir," Anton replied. "Treasure Hantz is thinking of suing you for breach of contract after you were photographed wearing a pair of shoes from a rival brand. General Mingus is threatening to—and I quote—'wring your neck' if you ever come near his daughter again. There was also a message from a girl called Rita Haphisatou? It was quite a long message, but essentially she said that you went out with her best friend after you broke up with her, and for that she called you in no uncertain terms 'a scumbag, a rascal, a rogue, and a great big baf—'"

"All right, thank you, Anton!" Ladi shouted, interrupting the butler.

The corridor was lined with art portraits and busts on small stone plinths. Zero couldn't help but admire them.

Camih squeezed his shoulder. "Welcome to our home, Zero. I hope you will come to see it as your home too. You're about to meet Mr. Gauche, the guildmaster. He has the final authority to let in new guild members."

Zero felt a prickle of panic. He had forgotten there was no guarantee that he would be accepted into Shango Heart. He imagined how embarrassing it would be to have traveled hundreds of thousands of miles only to be rejected. He swallowed thickly.

Camih must have seen the look of concern on his face because she added, "Don't worry. He is a very approachable guildmaster."

They went past a large atrium. Beautiful creepers climbed along the side of the walls and parts of the roof. At the center of the room was a great glass pillar fitted into a circular control panel. In the center of the pillar was projected an image of a man with an Afro, a septum ring, and black sunglasses. Above and below the face flashed a steady stream of information.

"This is the Job Hall," Camih explained. "Guild members can come here and look for any job they are interested in and register at the counter, provided they are of an appropriate rank to take it." She pointed to the far side of the room, where three marble counters were manned by elves in suits.

A group of four young children in matching gray pants and coats were huddled together by the counters, talking excitedly and darting looks at the glass pillar.

"Once they accomplish the mission, they will receive compensation in the form of oaths."

Zero had heard of the Sabas' currency—metal coins shaped like cowry. It was only accepted in special Saba establishments.

"What about the giant face?" asked Zero.

"Oh, that's Kodjo, the guild's supercomputer. Most guilds have one," said Ladi. "He manages the power supply and connects with the Intergalactic Saba Organization database. He is also impossible to beat at hologram chess. There's a ten-thousand-oath reward for any guild member who can beat him."

Ladi's voice was drowned out by a loud shout. A mechanical hand unfolded from an opening in the control panel. Zero watched as one of the children at the counters was pinned to the ground by the giant hand, unceremoniously picked up, shaken like a die, and then bowled right out of the atrium, knocking over his comrades like dominoes.

"You are not allowed to pick jobs you're not qualified for," explained Ladi, shaking his head.

They left the Job Hall and began navigating through what seemed like a dorm. As they walked down the corridor, some of the doors swung open and the heads of curious children poked out.

"This floor and the one above are the dorms for Sabins. The guild takes in children aged five and older. For many, this is their only home. Your dorm will be on the floor above. The third floor is reserved for the S-Class Sabas."

Zero's ears pricked up. He thought of the elusive third floor and began to imagine what incredible Sabas lived there, what Kobastickers they had . . .

"You will learn to use your Kobasticker after you meet with Mrs. Bigslow. She'll have a talk with you and you'll settle on classes that will be a prerequisite for your development. Classes on self-defense, galactic history, Kobasticker mastery, and brand management are compulsory."

A large crowd of children all wearing gray pants and long-sleeved shirts with high collars poured out of their rooms and gathered in the corridor. There was a hum of excited voices, and a few of them called out to Camih.

"Camih, is it true that you defeated Lenoir the aristocrat in a duel?"

"Camih, Camih, will you come and play levitation chess with us?"

Until behind them someone yelled, "Camih!"

Ladi froze, and Camih let out a groan.

Standing in the middle of the corridor was a pretty girl with her hair styled in sisterlocks, wearing bright yellow sneakers. She looked vaguely familiar. Her eyes sparked with intensity, her fingers were curled into fists, and her face was pinched in a scowl. She looked like a bull about to charge.

The children of stardust gave the girl a wide berth and looked anxiously to Camih.

"Soraya," growled Camih.

Zero looked to Ladi.

"Her sister," he whispered.

Zero's eyes bulged. He looked at the two girls, from the calm and composed Camih to the angry Soraya.

"I have come for my revenge. This time, I'll be victorious," said Soraya.

"You are setting yourself up to be sorely disappointed," said Camih.

Ladi let out a sigh and stepped between the two sisters.

"All right, it seems we are going to have another duel. Soraya Sitso is challenging Camih Sitso for the umpteenth time. As a reminder, this will be according to the Marquise of Iyanya Rules. Three Kobastickers max. Will the dueling parties put on their Saba gloves and wait for my signal?"

Zero watched as the two girls prepared.

Many of the children scuttled back inside their dorms. The corridor filled with the sound of doors being shut, one after the other like consecutive notes played on a xylophone. Zero saw Ladi take a step backward and decided to do the same.

Zero had heard of Saba duels but had never witnessed one before. An entrepreneurial young Sabin had begun to go down the corridor, taking bets. There was the sound of money changing hands.

The two girls stood facing each other with their eyes locked.

Ladi took it upon himself to explain Saba dueling etiquette to Zero.

"In Saba duels, it is good practice to materialize your Kobasticker and let your opponent see it."

As if on cue, the two girls bowed to each other and materialized their Kobastickers:

"*Koba-Reducenix,*" said Camih.

"*Koba-Blueflash,*" said Soraya.

Each sister's Kobasticker materialized with a tiny thunderclap.

"Ooh, it seems like Soraya is going for the kill. That's Blueflash, a powerful dueling Kobasticker," said Ladi knowingly.

Zero pointed at the Kobasticker Camih was holding.

"What Kobasticker does Camih have?"

"That's Reducenix. An irregular-type Kobasticker. You get hit by its ray and you'll shrink to one-tenth of your height for six hours."

The two sisters held their Kobastickers over the inside of their forearms.

Ladi shouted, "Go!"

There was a burst of activity. They both slapped their Kobastickers onto their skin.

Soraya was quicker.

"*Blueflash!*" she cried.

A beam of blue light shot across the corridor toward Camih.

Camih merely tilted her head to the side, the beam shooting past her face, illuminating it for a brief second with a pale blue glow.

It was Camih's turn.

"*Reducenix!*" she shouted. A bolt of yellow light struck

Soraya in the chest. Her mouth popped open like a fish freshly landed on the banks of a river. She fell onto her knees, her hands rising to her throat.

There was a loud *swoosh* noise, like a punctured balloon. Zero had the impression that the girl was falling before he realized that she was *shrinking*.

Soraya shrank to the size of a mouse. She let out a scream of anguish, but it sounded like she had swallowed helium. She turned and bolted down the corridor.

Ladi shook his head.

"That's her forty-sixth defeat in a row," he said.

There came a screech that sounded like nails on a chalkboard.

"Attention, guild members," a voice called from a loudspeaker overhead. "An emergency meeting has been called. All Sabins and Sabas are to report to the dining hall immediately. Thank you."

"That doesn't sound good," said Ladi.

Zero looked to Camih.

"It must be Mr. Gauche. He is probably going to fill us in on his meeting with the committee. Come on."

The dining hall was another atrium with glass floors, so that all around people appeared to be floating in space. A number of guild members sat in wicker basket chairs at circular tables covered with white cloths. The room was decorated with towering potted bamboo trees set between the tables. Electric lamps hung from the ceiling, basking them in a pale orange glow.

On the far side of the room, two important-looking people in sweeping white gowns and square hats sat at opposite ends of a large table. They looked at the assembled company with great dissatisfaction, including the person sitting in a great peacock chair next to their table, presiding over the whole room.

Mr. Gauche was a tall man dressed in a black coat with gold buttons and matching gold shoulder straps with gold tassels. He was perfectly normal from his legs to his neck, but where his head would have been there was a giant TV screen. From the screen, the head of a very large rabbit looked out at them.

"Have a seat, Zero," said Camih as they got to their table.

Zero sat down, unable to take his eyes off the guildmaster.

He finally cast a look around the room. He recognized a number of famous Sabas. There was Halima Getts. She stood out with her helmet. It looked like a deep-sea diver's, with four circular faceplates around it.

Halima had solved Okanwu's Law of Kobasticker Formation by age six, written a published paper about Kobasticker evolution in the *Intergalactical New Science Review* by age nine, and had joined Shango Heart despite being accepted to MEDUSA, the guild that recruited genius-level Sabas.

He spotted Amy Bigslow with her bright head scarf, blond hair, and patterned red-and-yellow dress. She was frequently on the Most Beautiful Sabas list and had ten million followers on Sigmia.

They were all dressed in Saba jackets, with the horizontal blue safety lines across them and the Shango Heart insignia embroidered on their shoulders.

Zero felt awe sweep through him like a tide. He had only seen these people on *Saba Now*. He suddenly felt incredibly small.

Zero caught sight of Soraya. She had still not returned to her original size and was sitting on a mountain of pillows. As if sensing his gaze, she looked at him full on, and Zero looked away quickly.

Mr. Gauche got to his feet. A chorus of shushes rippled through the room. Everyone fell silent except for a young Saba who was talking loudly to the boy next to him.

Mr. Gauche cleared his throat, but the poor Saba remained oblivious. Mr. Gauche took a deep breath and materialized a Kobasticker showing a hand with a gold bolt of energy shooting out of it. He pressed it against his forearm.

The Saba didn't even notice as the people around him—including the boy he was speaking to—scooted away from him. A bolt of golden light speared across the room and blasted the talking Saba off his feet, slamming him into the wall.

"Do I have your attention now?" asked Mr. Gauche, his Kobasticker still glowing.

Every single soul in the room gave a throaty "Yes, sir!"

"Excellent. Could somebody please take care of Octave?"

There was the shuffle of feet as a few Sabas picked up the boy. His hair was smoking and his eyes were rolling around wildly. They sat him back at his table.

"As you all know, today we have the honor of hosting two distinguished members of the Saba Guild Compliance Committee, Mr. Snodgrass and Mrs. Pumbleluck. They are responsible for all the guilds in the eighth quadrant of our galaxy. Please join me in welcoming them."

There was a smattering of cheers and then total silence.

The two committee members nodded stiffly, their eyes surveying the room.

"The outcome of our discussions I will share with you in time, but there is a particular issue I wished to address with you now in their presence.

"As we stand here on this day the twelfth of June, we face the astonishing number of three hundred and sixty-seven lawsuits. Thirty alone in the past month."

Zero shifted his feet under the table.

"This is by far the greatest number of cases against us and puts us in a very precarious position. And to make it worse, almost every single one of you is involved."

Mr. Gauche looked around the room before settling his gaze on Zero's table.

"Ladi, your most recent client claims that while you saved him from a goblin kidnapping ring, during the rescue you threw him down three stories and dragged him through a river infested with Neptunian two-headed crocodiles. He is suing for negligence and wanton endangerment and wants us to pay compensation for his hospital bills and for the psychiatric trauma."

Ladi sank lower in his chair.

"Octave Gurnani!"

The boy who had been blasted off his seat bolted upright as if he had sat on a nail.

"During a mission on the planet Ashokina, you were tasked with keeping the crown prince of the Uldrian empire safe from assassination attempts. The king claims he caught you barbecuing the royal pet chicken with sautéed plantains and yams. He is suing you for grave psychological violence."

Octave winced.

"Camih. A few dark guilds have complained about your use of excessive force when arresting their members. Not to mention the damage to a two-thousand-year-old temple on Anansi 12."

Camih smiled sheepishly at Zero.

"My fellow guild members: As Sabas, the work we do is of great importance. We have a rich history. In our early days, Sabas were explorers who sought out inhabitable planets, resources, and forms of energy. Today, Sabas perform a variety of duties and are something of the handymen of space: they uncover ancient ruins, piece together the history of humanity from the Blue Age to the present day, deliver important items across the galaxy, and even help keep the peace by arresting dangerous criminals and rescuing stranded space travelers. Sabas are both humanity's memory and its spear. We are the only thing protecting humanity from the creatures lurking in the Oblong Dimension and their ruler Zomon, who has tried countless times to destroy our galaxy.

"Sabas are an order of risk takers who strive to understand the universe in order to ensure humanity's continued survival. Once revered, today the Sabas face challenges that are growing greater by the day. The Intergalactic Space Government is restricting Saba licenses and cutting subsidies for guilds in response to a rise in anti-Saba sentiment. Many see the work we do as a waste of money and time. These people are content with the way things are. They have lost their curiosity and desire to explore and are happy to wither away in ignorance."

Looking all around the room, Zero saw that almost every face wore an expression of intense concentration. Despite the fact that he did not yet belong to the guild, he felt himself sucked into the collective emotion shared by every member at that precise moment.

"As Sabas, we must be aware of this reality. Our guild is a safe and welcoming environment where we teach young children of stardust how to master their Kobastickers. Here at Shango Heart we produce strong-willed, passionate Sabas with integrity. We are not the richest guild. We don't have a wealthy patron willing to bankroll us or lucrative sponsorship deals. We are independent, and our independence is our strength. Our results speak for themselves. Many Hearters have gone on to be incredibly successful Sabas. A few have become single-digit ranked Sabas."

Mr. Gauche sent his gaze roaming around the room.

"We are said to be rebellious, stubborn, and reckless by many so-called guild experts."

Mr. Snodgrass nodded approvingly. He raised a glass of wine to his lips and took a sip.

"But I say forget that!"

Mr. Snodgrass spat out his mouthful of wine.

"Be who you want to be!" Mr. Gauche cried. "Never apologize for who you are. Run wild! *That* is the Shango Heart way."

The two members of the regulation committee looked at Mr. Gauche, the shock plain on their faces.

Mr. Gauche was grinning now.

"I will never seek to muzzle the way you express yourselves. Those who hire us know what to expect. And I want you to know that no matter what happens, as long as you stay true to yourselves and true to the Shango Heart way, you will always have a defender in me! Goodbye and *bon appétit*."

Cheers exploded around the room. A number of guild members gave Mr. Gauche a standing ovation.

The two committee members looked like they had just swallowed tarantulas.

"Camih and Ladi, if we could please have a word. Thank you!"

And with that, Mr. Gauche got to his feet and exited the hall, the members of the regulation committee left gaping after him.

"That was epic!" said Zero as they left the main hall, the sounds of cheering guild members melting away.

"That was classic Mr. Gauche," replied Camih.

"Did he always have a television over his head?" asked Zero.

"He is from the planet Plexus. And all Plexarians look like that," said Camih.

Ladi nodded.

"At any rate, we're lucky to have Mr. Gauche. He was ranked as one of the top Sabas in the galaxy when he was younger," said Camih.

· ❄ · 🐙 · 🐙 · 🐊 · ⚱ · 🛸 · 🦟 · 🦗 · 🦠 · ✋ · 🎐 · ◬ ·

Mr. Gauche's office was the only office on the twelfth floor.

They stopped right outside the door, where a plaque read "Mr. Gauche—Shango Heart Guildmaster."

Camih opened the door and held it open for Zero.

It was a small office with a plush red carpet. On either side were glass-fronted bookshelves. In the middle of the room was a great mahogany desk with another peacock chair in which sat Mr. Gauche. His feet were on the table and his hands were steepled together. On the screen that was his head, a documentary showed migrating birds floating through the sky in a formation resembling the tip of an arrow. Then the channel changed and Zero was once again looking at the face of a rabbit.

Zero glanced inside the bookcases, which held countless artifacts from Planet Blue.

Mr. Gauche noticed Zero's gaze. "Collecting old technology from the ancient civilizations on Blue is a passion of mine."

Zero looked at Camih. She nodded, so he walked over to the case nearest him. Inside, a rectangular black object rested on a yellow cushion.

"That is an artifact called a 'VCR tape.' It is believed to have been used by inhabitants of Blue to decorate their walls, and occasionally as a method of self-defense. See the sharp sides and the thickness?"

Next to the glass cabinet with the VCR was another containing a white cardboard square that looked like it had been dropped in brackish water and then dried. It had the word "pizza" written on the front in black.

"This is called a 'pizza box' and was used to contain a thing called a pizza. It is thought to be a culinary weapon of some kind. Inhabitants of Blue would send them to their enemies in the hope that they would grow fat and perish. The jury is out on why people would willingly eat anything so unhealthy. Although it seems that culinary warfare was quite prevalent, given the wealth of unhealthy foods available."

Zero's attention was drawn to another glass cabinet, where on a small television screen a pretty woman with pale skin was painting her face.

"That is a recording of a practice common on Blue. I bought it off an elven salesman in the Delta asteroid belt. It was common for women to wear elaborate war paint on their faces. Some variations would take as much as seven hours to complete. Historians believe they would shave their eyebrows and paint them back on. It might have served two purposes: scaring away predators or annoying suitors, and hiding from tax collectors."

Zero stared at the video of a woman applying copious quantities of paste to her face, a generous layer of red paint to her lips, and blue powder to her eyes.

Mr. Gauche cleared his throat. "My dear friends, please have a seat."

They did as they were told.

"Is this the new recruit?" Mr. Gauche asked, nodding at Zero.

"Yes, sir," Camih replied.

"From Anansi 12?"

"Yes, sir," Ladi answered.

"Fantastic."

On Mr. Gauche's face, the rabbit disappeared and was replaced with black-and-white images of children dancing in a classroom. Zero supposed the channels on the television changed depending on his mood. Talking with Mr. Gauche was awkward. As he had no face, Zero had the impression that he was talking to no one, the guildmaster's voice seeming to come from everywhere at once.

"You want to become a Saba, my lad? You want to follow the path that Zoe did many years before?"

"There is nothing I would like more than to become a Saba," Zero said earnestly.

Mr. Gauche nodded.

"As I said before, our guild is always open to any child of stardust who wishes to learn the arts of the Shango Heart way. You have come all the way here, and provided you pass the trial, you will join our family."

Zero felt as if a knife were pressed against his heart.

"Trial, sir?"

"We must duel, you and I. If you win, you get to join Shango Heart. If you lose, you go home."

Zero stared blankly at Mr. Gauche, trying to detect some levity in his voice. There was none. On the screen that was his face, the channel had changed to black-and-white footage of two boxers circling each other in a ring.

"Are you ready?"

Zero's worst fears were realized. A duel against a guildmaster. If he lost, he was going home.

"I will use a simple stun Kobasticker," Mr. Gauche continued. "Third class. The duel will follow the Duke of St. Barthelemy Rules."

Zero turned to look at Camih and Ladi. Their faces were impassive; there would be no help from those quarters.

Mr. Gauche rolled up his sleeves. He towered over Zero. Out the window, Zero saw a stray taxi whizzer dissect the starry sky.

Zero could barely materialize his Kobasticker.

"To make things fair, I will let you start," Mr. Gauche said. "What do you say?"

He spread his arms like a speaker basking in a standing ovation. Camih and Ladi stepped to the side of the room.

Zero swallowed.

He reached out and touched the inside of his wrist with two trembling fingers and said "*K-k-koba-Jupiter.*"

Please don't embarrass yourself, he thought, shutting his eyes tightly.

Zero felt a prickle of electricity move along his arm. His palm began to itch, and he opened his eyes in time to see a miniature spark shoot from his palm and fizzle out a foot in front of him.

Zero smiled sheepishly.

"My turn," said Mr. Gauche. A handsome, grinning man appeared on the television screen.

Zero barely had enough time to prepare himself. A Kobasticker glowed on the back of Mr. Gauche's forearm without him saying a word.

He aimed a bolt of red energy at Zero, and it struck him on the collarbone, blasting him off his feet. Zero landed heavily on the floor, unable to move. The realization that he had lost and what it meant for his dreams swept over him like a dark tide. He felt a knot in the back of his throat and hot tears gathering behind his eyelids. He slowly sat up, his hand pressed against the spot where the spell had struck him. It didn't burn as much when he pressed his palm against it.

And then Mr. Gauche said, "Well done, Zero."

Zero looked up at him, confused.

"Take a look at your collarbone." Mr. Gauche inclined his head toward him.

Zero lifted the collar of his shirt. Glowing on his skin was the emblem of Shango Heart: a round mask with white eyes, two thick vertical lines running down the middle, and three slanted lines in the space under each eye. He looked from Mr. Gauche to Camih and Ladi. They were all grinning at him.

"Welcome to Shango Heart, Zero," murmured Camih.

CHAPTER 9

"HOW crazy was that?" asked Camih excitedly, once they were outside Mr. Gauche's office.

"Does he always do something that theatrical every time a new person joins the guild?" Zero asked.

"Of course. For Octave, Mr. Gauche challenged him to eat a five-pound cake in five minutes. The stamp with the guild emblem was hidden inside the cake. Except Octave ate it all, including the stamp."

"We knew he was pulling your leg, bud. We just couldn't say anything," said Ladi, winking at him.

· 🎲 · 🐙 · 🐡 · 🧍 · 🏺 · 🍲 · 🐜 · 🦗 · 🧸 · ✋ · 🎏 · 🔺 ·

The first days of Zero's life as a Saba were spent getting used to the uniqueness of life in Shango Heart. Shango Heart was an incredible guild with a host of larger-than-life characters and creatures. Zero learned about Biscotte, the guild's mascot and resident invisible dog. Biscotte had eaten an invisibility Kobasticker someone had left lying around and was now an invisible licking machine and tripping hazard. More than once, Zero found himself inexplicably bulldozed and subjected to an onslaught of licks.

There were also the almost-daily duels between Camih and Soraya. These were usually announced by shouts of

"They're at it again!" followed by guild members ducking for cover to avoid being caught in the crossfire. On his third day, Zero had found himself rushing back from one of the vending machines with his arms full of packs of plantain chips and a sugar bun poking out of his mouth as he dodged multiple beams of Blueflash.

But there were also all the perks of being a Sabin. Zero got a Shango Heart starter kit that included a Goooober, a diary, his Shango Heart Sabin ID card, and a Sabin jacket. Ladi took the time to show Zero the juice bar, which was open twenty-four hours a day and was managed by a friendly djinn called Cici. Zero spent a lot of time asking her about her suppliers and her business model. There was even a massage parlor.

There was also Anton and the guild's lawyer, Mr. Hernandez.

"But he's currently on leave," Ladi explained.

"What happened?" Zero asked curiously.

"He suffered a mental breakdown working for the guild."

But the thing that surprised Zero the most was his popularity in the guild.

Part of it had to do with his sneakers, the Abalo 12s. As Zero walked around, many of the Sabins would gawk at them. It turned out that they were extremely rare and were considered masterpieces of their creator, the mercurial Boris Abalo.

And part of it had to do with Camih and Ladi. All the kids wanted to be like them—famous young Sabas with their own whizzer. They were incredibly popular, and since Camih and Ladi had decided to be Zero's mentors, that made

Zero the object of the other apprentices' fascination. Zero loved hanging out with Camih and Ladi, and he valued their opinions. More than anyone he had known before, he wanted them to think well of him. He wanted to make them proud.

Zero was staring at the electronic bulletin board next to the entrance to the dining hall when a poster caught his attention. Among the advertisements for a Saba exchange program with a guild called Blue Minotaur and a whizzer piloting school run by elves, there was a poster of a human silhouette inside a red circle with a line through it. The silhouette seemed oddly familiar. It looked strangely like . . .

"Octave," said Ladi.

"I don't understand, he is forbidden from . . . ?"

"Reciting poetry. It's a guild-wide ban. Although if you ask me, his rapping and his stand-up sets are just as dangerous," said Ladi.

Zero said nothing but wondered how bad a person's poetry skills had to be that they could be banned from reciting their work.

He quickly found out why.

Knowing that new members would be less likely to be aware of the ban, Octave sought out Zero and begged for a chance to recite some poetry for him.

Zero obliged, his curiosity piqued. They holed themselves up in Zero's dorm that night after dinner. Octave shone bright with eagerness at finally having someone he could recite to.

Octave cleared his throat.

"This poem is called 'Reflections in a Bubble on Venus under the Light of a 35-Volt Ceiling Lamp.'"

"That's pretty specific."

"It captures the mood I was in when I wrote it."

"Sure. Let's hear it . . ."

Zero made it through two lines of Octave's poem before he begged him to stop reciting.

"Did that one not suit your fancy?" Octave asked, concerned. "I could perform another, if you'd like? Perhaps 'Meaningful Meditations on a Beach on Jupiter'—"

"No! And please don't insist or I might throw this desk lamp at you."

When Zero told Ladi that Octave's poem had been so bad that he'd just barely resisted the urge to whack Octave across the head, Ladi was not at all surprised.

"That's exactly why he has been forbidden from reciting his poems, bud. They are so bad they cause a bloodlust in all who hear them. I once heard of a race of aliens called the Bubuskas who would go into battle reciting special poems that turned them into killing machines. I think he has some Bubuska in him."

"Poor Octave. He must feel terrible at not having anyone he can recite his poems to," said Zero.

They were in the dining hall, digging into a plate of grilled plantains, coconut rice, and peanut sauce. Camih was on a video call with the company that sponsored her whizzer.

"Before the ban, we had a talent show once and Octave recited a poem. We ended up with thirteen members in the hospital following his performance. Three of them tried to knock themselves out by banging their heads against the tables. One was in critical condition after he tried to swallow his own shoe. Mr. Gauche placed the ban shortly after."

Ladi took a huge bite of plantain before changing the subject. "How are your lessons going? Everybody in the guild has been raving about you. They say you're a sponge, absorbing knowledge quicker than they've ever seen."

Zero felt heat rise to his face.

"Lessons are going pretty well," he admitted, "although I haven't been able to start a few classes, like Saba History and Detectives Skills. But Rune Reading and Ancient Languages is one of my favorites, and so is Beast Studies."

"What about Media, Communications, and Branding?"

"It's been . . . all right," said Zero thoughtfully. "It's been a bit hard to wrap my head around all the things I have to do to market myself as a Saba."

Ladi nodded.

"Yes, but trust me, you will be glad you did. Mrs. Bigslow knows what she's doing. She is a wizard when it comes to helping Sabas market themselves. Not too long ago, a rumor started that I was going out with Camih."

Zero almost choked on his mango juice.

"She told us to lean into it for a while, to neither deny nor confirm. That really grew our following and our platform," said Ladi matter-of-factly.

"And, er . . . were you?"

"Was I what?" he asked around a mouthful of fufu.

Zero struggled to say the words.

"Going out."

"Oh that! No, we're just friends, bud," said Ladi, smiling.

Zero felt relief wash over him.

"Who are just friends?" said a voice.

Zero turned to see Camih and Octave standing beside them, holding trays overflowing with food. They sat down.

"Zero was asking me if you and I were going out."

Zero's eyes flew open. He glared at Ladi, but he just grinned back.

"Oh did he?" she asked, looking at Zero curiously. Her eyes were bright with mischief.

"How was your call with your whizzer sponsor?" asked Ladi.

"It went all right. Although I couldn't understand much on account of the fact that he was bawling. The *Ladybug* was apparently an expensive prototype, but he promised to repair it and send me another Kobasticker to summon it."

"So all is well then," said Zero.

"You could say that. What were you guys talking about?" she asked.

"I was telling him about Mrs. Bigslow," said Ladi.

"Have you started Media, Communications, and Branding?" asked Camih, turning to Zero.

Zero nodded.

"What Saba profile did Mrs. Bigslow tell you to go for?" asked Octave.

"Well, she supposes that I should go for 'innocent boy

next door.' She figures I can gain an edge from the guild's rebelliousness and rough image by being the innocent guy everyone wants to root for. She said that I need to be really selective about the missions I choose to accept. I should go for object and Kobasticker retrieval missions."

He thought about the other Saba stereotypes she had mentioned. She had called Ladi's type "the loverboy"—he exploited his good looks and charm. Camih was "the rose in the concrete."

"What did she say my type was?" asked Octave, ripping the flesh from a turkey leg with his teeth.

"I think she said you were the guild mascot," lied Zero. When Zero had asked Mrs. Bigslow about Octave, she'd said that some people in the guild were there to make the others look better by comparison.

Zero looked down at his watch.

"You have something to attend?" asked Ladi.

"I have to go see Halima. She asked me to drop by so she can fit me with some Saba gloves."

"A word of advice then: Don't touch anything in her lab," Camih said, her face serious. "I mean it."

· 🕸 · 🐙 · 🐙 · 🙆 · ✋ · 🍲 · 👾 · 🐜 · 👹 · ✋ · 🔖 · 🔺 ·

When Zero arrived at Halima's office, just as he reached out to knock, a loud explosion from within the room made the whole building shake. The door opened and a wall of green smoke rolled over Zero, making him cough.

"Who's there?" called a voice from inside.

"It's Zero!"

"Come in."

Zero held his breath and stepped into the green vapor. As the cloud settled, he caught a glimpse of Halima. She was standing behind a metal plinth, a Kobasticker bobbing in the air above her releasing green smoke.

Halima was flanked by two Geekaloos in lab coats wielding clipboards.

"Glad you could make it. I just wanted to monitor your Kobasticker and give you your Kobagloves."

Zero gawked at Halima. Through the faceplate, a girl with frizzy hair and big inquisitive eyes stared out at him.

"Apologies. I was repairing a fossil that was brought in yesterday," she said, removing her helmet and sniffing some of the green smoke.

"Fossil?" asked Zero.

"Fossils are Kobastickers that have not been used in a very long time, sometimes in thousands of years. After that long, they tend to turn to stone. Getting them back into working shape can be quite a drawn-out process. Follow me."

He followed Halima through a bulkhead door in the back of her office, into another room with dozens of electronic plinths where a number of Kobastickers were floating in beams of white light.

"These are interesting Kobastickers you have here," said Zero, trying to make conversation.

"Yes, I suppose."

"What does this one do?" asked Zero, pointing to the one nearest him. It was a Kobasticker showing a bald face with its tongue out and fancy symbols surrounding it.

"That's a Kobasticker that lets you speak a dead language called Creole."

"Nice!" Zero reached forward to touch it.

"But then it gives you a heart attack and you die. So I wouldn't touch it."

Zero's finger curled like a sheet of paper held too close to a fire. He pulled his hand back, smiling sheepishly.

"What about this one?" he asked, nodding at a hexagonal Kobasticker with a sun symbol in the center.

"That one is an irregular type. It lets you see about ten seconds into the future. It causes mild migraines, though."

"Is it safer than the previous one?"

"Not really, because after the migraines clear up, you die."

"Ah . . . and what about this one?" asked Zero, pointing to a circular Kobasticker with a sword in the center flanked by two dragon skulls. He was desperate to find one he could use.

"That one, you just die."

Zero took a very big step backward, trying to put as much distance as possible between him and the Kobasticker.

They made their way to the back of the room, where a large control panel took up the whole wall. Metal grates covered the floor and cables ran everywhere. On a table to Zero's right, several Kobastickers encased in an amber-like substance were wrapped in thick padded blankets as if they had just come in from a snowstorm.

A few Geekaloos in lab coats were aiming a very large speaker at one of the amber-encased Kobastickers, like barbers holding up a mirror to a client's head after a haircut. Another Geekaloo was taking notes and inspecting the fossil. The speaker was blaring a song, the noise causing the air inside the room to pulse.

Zero looked from the Geekaloos to Halima, confusion written all over his face.

"They are hatching a fossil. 'No Leftovers' by the hip-hop artist Big Chubz has been shown to reverse the effects of fossilization on Kobastickers when played loud enough," she said, as if that explained everything.

Halima gave instructions to one of the Geekaloos and it hurried out of the room, returning with a black container.

She took it and opened it in front of Zero. Inside was a pair of large black gloves, with the Shango Heart logo embroidered on the backs.

"These Saba gloves are made from stardust from the exploded star Ortix, and are laced with Durahilcon, which will conduct electricity and be perfect for lightning-based Kobastickers. The inside is padded in wool from sheep raised on Saturn. You can have a try."

Zero rubbed his hands before reaching for the gloves and trying them on. There was a slight tingle as he slid them over his hands. He could almost feel an electric pulse traveling through them. He wriggled his fingers.

The Geekaloos took some measurements of Zero's body with strange mechanical sensors. When they were finished, they wrote on their clipboards and handed them to Halima.

"How have your Koba lessons been going?" she asked, tucking the clipboards behind her back.

Zero raised one shoulder.

"Can you list the seven main types of Kobastickers and their shapes?"

"Easy. Summoning types help materialize objects and creatures, and they are square in shape. Skill-type Kobastickers allow the user to master a skill or acquire knowledge, and they're shaped like triangles. Transformation types morph the user into a creature or an animal and are kite shaped, and elemental types are circles . . ."

Zero tried to remember the last ones, but they were swimming out of reach of his memory.

"Medicine types contain healing spells and support-type Kobastickers are all those that amplify or modify the way other Kobastickers work. They're shaped like rhombuses," said Zero.

"And irregular types?"

"Rarer. They contain all the Kobastickers with abilities that do not fit inside the main six types. They have a hexagonal shape."

"Good. What are the four classes of Kobastickers?"

"Regular Kobastickers are the most common and can be used by Nevits," said Zero, using the name for non-Saba people. "After that there are the superstickers, the megastickers, and the ultrastickers, which are the rarest and most powerful Kobastickers, made from magic spanning galaxies."

"Any exceptions to this system of classification?"

Zero racked his brain. There were so many, and he often got them confused.

"Give me two," prodded Halima.

"The Uranus Kobasticker. All the other Origin-series Kobastickers are considered superstickers, but Uranus is considered an ultrasticker."

"That's right, Uranus is locked away in the headquarters of the Intergalactic Space Government and is considered a magical weapon of mass destruction. Any others?"

"Andromeda?" offered Zero. "The Constellation series are considered superstickers too, but Andromeda is considered a megasticker."

"That works. It is very important that you be able to identify the different classes of Kobastickers and know the exceptions. You don't want to be in a duel and find out you underestimated a Kobasticker your opponent is using!"

"If I gave you a Kobasticker called Firenix, how would you use it?"

"That's easy. I would materialize it using the words *Koba-Firenix*. Then I'd place it on my forearm and say the name of the Kobasticker, in this case *Firenix*, to activate it."

Halima made a noise of satisfaction. "Not bad. Your knowledge is coming along nicely."

There was a loud shriek behind Zero. He turned around and saw that one of the fossils had been cracked open. A baby dragon with big, lidded eyes and an oversized head jumped out and proceeded to fasten its mouth around the nearest Geekaloo's blue finger. The poor Geekaloo leapt into the air and ran in circles trying to dislodge the dragon. Its colleagues gave chase to help.

Halima shook her head. "A dragon egg. It is quite common

for wily goblin traders to disguise dragon eggs as fossils. A very lucrative business for them."

The Geekaloos were now trying to yank the young dragon off their companion's finger while avoiding the little bursts of flames coming from the creature's nostrils. The baby dragon finally relented, only to bite the nose of the nearest Geekaloo. The chaos continued.

"How are you getting along with your Jupiter?" Halima asked, as if nothing were happening.

"That's just it, Halima. It's been a nightmare learning to use it."

"Why don't you materialize it so I can see? Use your new Saba gloves."

Zero put on the gloves and held out his hand, his palm facing up. He shut his eyes and tried to materialize Jupiter.

Koba-Jupiter, he breathed.

The Jupiter appeared in a swirl of gold sparks above his palm. The thunderbolt at the planet's center seemed to glow.

"Here goes nothing," mumbled Zero. He plucked the bobbing Kobasticker out of the air and pressed it onto his forearm. He felt his skin grow cold beneath it.

A growing ball of electricity began to build in the pit of his stomach like a roiling mass of bees. Zero tried to wrest some control over this growing ball of energy inside him, to no avail. The ball grew until it exploded, sending bolts of electricity surging through his body.

Against this onslaught of energy, his mind was like a clump of mud in the path of rushing water. He felt his consciousness slipping away. In his mind's eye he saw a lake bordered by a ring of dead trees. In the center of the lake was a giant baobab tree. But it was unlike any tree he had ever seen.

Every branch held television screens instead of leaves.

A man in a flowing white kaftan, his face veiled in shadows, sat on one of the branches.

"That's enough now."

When Zero came to, he was lying on his back on the floor of the laboratory. Wreaths of smoke surrounded his head.

Halima was staring at him, a frown of concentration on her face.

"How can I learn to master it and not die in the process?" Zero asked her.

"There is no easy answer to that. The path to mastering a Kobasticker involves many variables. Some have to do with the Saba in question. Concentration, a desire to perpetually learn—these are important qualities for a Saba. Imagination, too, is important. Using their imagination, Sabas are able to put their Kobastickers to all kind of uses and tap into all types of fantastic abilities."

"But I have been trying all these things. What am I doing wrong?"

Halima was looking at him carefully, as if she wasn't sure how much of what she would say next he would understand.

"In some cases, the Kobastickers themselves might not want you to succeed. That might be what is happening here."

"I'm not sure I understand," said Zero, confused.

"You see, Kobastickers are not simple tools to be used as you please. Every time a person uses a Kobasticker, they leave behind a bit of themselves that molds it. Over time, these Kobastickers grow more powerful. Some evolve. Legacy Kobastickers and ultrastickers such as the Zodiacs . . . many of these are so powerful because they have been around for millennia. But after so many users, these Kobastickers have also developed something of a personality that is a collage of all their past users.

"I fear that this may be what you are grappling with. Learning to use a Kobasticker at its full potential is a deeply personal journey. But for now, I can recommend a few books to help you learn how to hone your skills."

Halima fished a notepad and pencil from her coat pockets and scribbled something on the paper before handing it to Zero.

"Here. This should help. You can find all these books in the guild library."

Zero nodded. Then a question popped into his mind.

"Will I be able to use other Kobastickers?"

"Of course. No doubt in time you will master many different Kobastickers."

"How will I know which ones to get?"

"The question we all ask ourselves. Some you will decide to acquire; others will find you. You will have the most compatibility with Kobastickers that fit your personality. Each Saba will have an affinity with certain Kobastickers."

Zero then asked a question he'd been holding onto for days now.

"What Kobasticker does Camih have?"

Halima glanced at him curiously. "Over the years, she

has come to possess a number of Kobastickers. Some she has bought, many she has found."

There was a sharp buzzing sound, and Halima looked down at her Goooober.

"My dear Zero, I am afraid I will have to leave you. I need to be somewhere in five minutes."

"Okay," said Zero, slightly crestfallen. He had been enjoying chatting with her.

Halima accompanied him back to the room with the green-smoke Kobasticker.

Just as Zero was about to leave the office, he turned and said, "Earlier you implied that my Kobasticker's personality might be working against me."

Halima blanched. "Did I say that?" she asked sheepishly.

"Why would my Kobasticker try to sabotage me?"

"The phenomenon is not uncommon. It's called Belligerent Kobasticker Syndrome," she explained.

"You have been getting quite close to Camih and Ladi." Halima looked at him meaningfully.

"Er . . . yes," said Zero, wondering what Halima was driving at.

"Those two are considered the brightest stars in our guild. Both are four-star Sabas. All the children of stardust admire them."

Zero said nothing, hoping his silence would create a vacuum she would try to fill. Behind Halima, the Geekaloos were all in a groaning pile in the other room. The baby dragon stalked around them, nibbling at dangling limbs.

Halima finally sighed. "Camih is your mentor, but you must not know ... Before you, Jupiter belonged to her boyfriend, Detz. He passed away a few years ago."

Zero felt as if a bucket of arctic water had drenched his body.

"It must be strange for her to be mentoring the successor to the Kobasticker that once belonged to him," said Halima. "I suppose Jupiter must not be too happy to see you getting close to her."

CHAPTER 10

DESPITE Zero's best efforts, Halima's words affected him like an explosion.

Camih had had a boyfriend, and he was one of the previous owners of Jupiter.

Naturally, Zero went to the guild library and tried to pull up as much information on Detz as he could from the Seeker archives. He found nothing. In fact, there was precious little on previous users of the Jupiter.

Over the next few days, Zero found himself wanting to ask Camih about Detz, but whenever they met, Zero backed away from his questions like a diver from the edge of a cliff, afraid of what they might uncover.

Seeing Zero every day must have been terrible for her. He would have been a reminder of what she had lost. Zero wondered if she ever compared the two of them.

He asked the librarian, an elf called Mrs. Blinx, for articles, books, and holotomes on Belligerent Kobasticker Syndrome.

Halima was right—it was quite common. He read about a particularly harrowing case in which a young whizzer pilot stole a Kobasticker from his rival. The Kobasticker was meant to improve his reflexes, but when he used it, it glued his foot to the accelerator and he crashed into an asteroid.

There seemed to be no cure for the condition. Some researchers argued for a diet of onion juice and carrots for a week, but Zero thought he would rather be electrocuted than have to go through that.

He found the books Halima had recommended. There was *Jupiter: Fifty Recorded Instances of Its Use and a Detailed Breakdown of Its Capabilities* by Jeffrey Toobin, and *Masters of Storm: A Comprehensive History of Lightning-Based Kobastickers* by Jemima Okaku. He learned breathing exercises to help his concentration and a wide range of spells for lightning-based Kobastickers.

But try as he might, the only ability he seemed to master was "shock-yourself-three-quarters-to-death," and it consisted of him sending a large current through his own body and knocking himself unconscious.

Thankfully, there was something to help him keep his mind off things.

"Happy Intergalactic Zodiac Day!" cried Octave one morning a few weeks later, as Zero was coming back from the showers.

Octave was wearing an oversized brown coat, round sunglasses, and a blond wig. He grinned at Zero.

"Huh?" Zero asked.

"Today we celebrate the Zodiac Sabas. It's a public holiday."

"Is that why everyone is wearing costumes?"

Octave nodded.

"Most people are dressed like Zoe and Kadj, our very own Zodiac Sabas. Zoe is Sagittarius, of course, and Kadj was Pisces."

"Who are you dressed as?"

"Marlo Gaza, the Taurus Zodiac," he replied, spinning around so Zero could see his whole costume.

Octave was right—Shango Heart went all out to honor their very own Zodiacs.

All day, the juice bar served passion fruit juice, which was Kadj's favorite. A charity raffle was organized for the restoration of old Maniki temples throughout the eighth quadrant of the galaxy, one of Zoe's passion projects.

Zero had never heard of Zodiac Day, and yet he was proud to see how popular his mentor was.

The children took turns playing Zoe and Kadj battling against the Space Force.

The whole manor was decorated, and almost every guild member wore a kente bandanna or a straw hat to commemorate Zoe and Kadj. It was a day to celebrate the Sabas fighting for freedom all across the galaxy.

That afternoon, after another failed attempt at using Jupiter, Zero decided to go to the juice bar to get himself a hibiscus smoothie. Cici looked at him suspiciously as she handed him his juice, and Zero realized that little bolts of electricity still flashed across his skin.

He was on his way to the dining hall when he noticed a fair bit of commotion outside Halima's office. A thick band of guild members were massed in front of her door, shouting loudly. Quite a few of them were holding up large onions.

Zero walked over and tapped a guild member at the edge of the crowd on the shoulder.

"What's going on?" he asked.

"It's Halima, my brother. She has used a Kobasticker that has turned all the food in the guild into onions!" he said, holding up one.

Zero moved through the crowd until he found himself standing next to Camih. She was wearing both a straw hat and a kente bandanna around her neck.

She turned and smiled at him.

"Happy Zoe and Kadj Day," she cheered.

Zero felt heat rise to his face.

"The very same to you."

"What are you up to right now?"

"Nothing."

"Perfect. There's something I want to show you."

They left the crowd just as Mr. Gauche arrived wearing a large hairnet that covered his television's antennas and holding a brown head of onion. On his screen, a battle between a pack of lions and a pack of hyenas was being broadcast.

"Halima!" he yelled. "What is going on? Please reverse this spell this minute! My mother's banana cake is gone! Halima?" He banged his fists against the office door.

Zero and Camih walked in silence for a while. The questions Zero wanted to ask her hung over him like tree branches.

Who was Detz? Was Camih being so nice to Zero just because he reminded her of Detz? Could Zero ever measure up to him?

Zero finally mustered the courage and was about to open

his mouth when the sound of padded footsteps barreled toward them. Something bulldozed over two guild members down the hall, sending them flying like bowling pins.

"Biscotte!" scolded Camih. And sure enough, Zero heard the familiar bark of the guild mascot as he hurried past them.

The two guild members got to their feet, swearing darkly under their breaths. They picked up the items they'd been holding and continued on their way.

And just like that, they had reached the reading room. Zero's window of opportunity had passed.

Camih let him in and closed the door behind them. The reading room was small but cozy, with lush carpets, mahogany bookshelves, and plush velvet armchairs. A massive chandelier hung from the hammerbeam ceiling. A writing table was pressed against a diamond-paned window overlooking the wide expanse of space.

Zero saw a space capsule decorated with bright lights come to an abrupt stop outside the manor. The capsule bloomed like a flower to reveal a stage complete with drums, a piano, and some guitars. Zero watched as a group of musicians in space suits popped out of a trapdoor in the center of the stage and took their places. The band began to play a furious tune as a video projector sent a beam of light shooting up into space above them. The projection showed a picture of a blue-skinned man with two antennas drooping from his forehead and the words "Krodeck, the galaxy's greatest jerk."

"What is going on?" Zero asked Camih, pointing at the show.

"That's a Rototorian caravan. You've never seen one?"

Zero shook his head.

"You basically pay a group of traveling musicians to embarrass someone. You tell them your issue with the person, and the group travels through space, stopping wherever there is a crowd, to play rude songs and project shameful videos about the victim. If the Rototorians are touched by your story, they might even do it for free."

Zero chuckled. "I see."

The two of them sat at the writing table.

"I've been meaning to speak to you," Camih said, suddenly serious. She handed him a rolled-up newspaper from her jacket pocket.

Zero saw the headline.

1,000 DAYS SINCE LAST SIGNS OF LIFE

He felt a thread of disquiet unspool in his belly.

"Read it."

"*It has been one thousand days since the expedition manned by Zoe Sitso last gave signs of life. The expensive expedition had been assembled through a partnership between the Intergalactic Space Government and the Intergalactic Saba Organization. Unfortunately, the ISO lost contact with the space shuttle nearly two weeks into the mission.*

"*The press secretary for the ISO says they still hold out hope. 'We will not turn our backs on the mission yet. There are myriad reasons why we might not have heard from them. We have the utmost trust in the people on this voyage. They constitute some of the most distinguished and competent people in their fields.'*

"*Not all intergalactic citizens share this view. 'This is just another blatant waste of money by the ISO, and I am not at all surprised. Sabas are relics of an archaic way of life. We are not explorers anymore. We need to focus our resources on taking care of the planets where we are currently living. We need to stop pouring money into these ridiculous missions and promoting these outlaws who frankly are threats to our society,' says Ginorio Cavanani, an accountant working on the planet Kpankakan."*

Camih placed a hand on his shoulder, startling him. He looked up at her, feeling the burn of tears in his eyes.

"Do you think she's . . . ?" he asked, his voice cracking.

It seemed impossible. Zoe had always been such a vivacious person. The idea that she was not alive, that she was not spreading her infectious good humor and positivity throughout the galaxy, was unthinkable.

Zero wiped away his tears with the back of his arm. He couldn't imagine how Camih was feeling. Zoe was her sister.

They sat in silence, the newspaper lying on the table between them. Outside, the Rototorian caravan had finished their first set. Zero watched as a few band players fidgeted with the projector. It now showed the face of a handsome man with violet skin and intense eyes. Superimposed over his face was a circle with a line through it, and above his head were the words "Christopher, also a jerk . . ."

"What was it like having Zoe as an older sister?" Zero asked quietly.

Camih smiled softly. "Not very different from the relationship I have with Soraya, actually. I used to be so unruly. I think I've always been a bit jealous of Zoe's ability to draw people to her. People would fawn over her, and it had little to do with her accomplishments or her status, which was something I realized only later. She was just such a genuine and kind person. And very determined. I think a part of me wanted to be like her, but I feared that as long as she was there, I'd never surpass her."

Zero nodded. Zoe formed a drawbridge between them. As they talked, they summoned her, making her memory materialize in the room like a snowman they were building together.

"Did you love her?" asked Camih after a while.

Zero felt his face grow hot.

"N-no, of course not. She was just my mentor. She was much older anyway," he said quickly, grasping at whatever excuse he could find.

"I'm older than you," she said, a glint in her eye, "and I'm your mentor."

There was a knock on the door. Zero could have kissed whoever had thought to interrupt this embarrassing moment.

Octave poked his head into the room.

"Er . . . guys, someone is here to see you. A lawyer type."

Zero looked to Camih. A shadow had come over her face.

"Tell them to meet us in the waiting room," she replied.

· 🔷 · 🐙 · 🦑 · 👽 · ✋ · 🛸 · 🔭 · 🐜 · 🗿 · ✋ · 🎴 · ◎ ·

The meeting room was a small chamber next to the lobby. A giant portrait of Mr. Gauche hung on a wall, and some antique sofas and lamps were placed around the room. Mr. Gauche himself was there waiting for them. The screen that was his face showed a tiger sleeping in a rectangle of sunlight on the floor of a study. When Zero and Camih entered, the channel changed to a familiar handsome face.

Beside Mr. Gauche, seated at a round glass table, was a gentle-looking man with spectacles, and eyes that were slitted and yellow like a cat's. Next to him, resting on the table, was a golden chest.

Mr. Gauche spoke first.

"Camih and Zero, I would like to present Mr. Prevalence Jenkins, a lawyer who represents Zoe and who would like to have a word with you."

Zero nodded. He felt his heart beat a little faster.

"Thank you, Mr. Gauche," the man said calmly before turning to Zero and Camih. "I am a lawyer at Jenkins & Jenkins & Jenkins. I am here as the executor of Ms. Zoe Sitso's estate. Now, before you panic, I must insist that this is not in any way a pronouncement on Zoe's current . . . state of health. However, Ms. Sitso did take certain preventative measures in the event that she disappeared for a significant period of time—in particular, one thousand days."

He walked back to the golden chest and pressed some numbers on a keypad on the lid. There was some clicking and then a hiss as the lid unfolded.

"There are some objects Zoe asked that we deliver to her disciples and members of her family. Mr. Gauche allowed me to see Ms. Soraya a few moments ago."

Mr. Jenkins removed a piece of paper from his inner pocket. "*To Camih,*" he read, "*an unfinished draft of our mother's last book of poetry, so that it may remind you of her,*" he said.

·

He pulled out a leather-bound manuscript, which he handed to Camih.

"To Zero, a picture we took together. Continue to be the incredible young man you are, and never lose your curiosity."

He handed a framed picture to Zero.

Zero took it with trembling hands. He looked at the scrawny young boy flanked by a beautiful Zoe and Kadj. He remembered that day. It had been not long after they finally managed to repair their whizzer. Zoe had insisted on them taking a picture before they left.

Zero felt a sharp pain in his throat.

"Furthermore, Zoe has created an Nka addressed to her disciples. Do you know what an Nka is?"

"A method of encryption," Zero answered. "Sabas use Nkas when they need to pass on information or valuable property. They're treasure hunts that weed out untrustworthy or unworthy people."

"Precisely. Sabas set up an Nka as a sort of will so they can give their estate or pass on any outstanding missions to a worthy Saba. The candidate can only inherit the Saba's estate when they prove themselves worthy by accomplishing the trial set for them. I believe at this point it would be better if I let the beneficiary of the Nka speak for herself."

The sound of someone clearing their throat filled the room.

One moment the seat next to Mr. Jenkins was empty, and the next a tall, pretty woman was sitting in it.

"Chuksapanza!" cried Zero and Camih in unison.

The stranger had purple hair styled in a Mohawk and a strong face. She had blue-tinted skin and a white horn that protruded from her forehead like an ivory finger. When she spoke, her eyes crinkled.

"My name is Selima Turkoglu, heiress to the Turkoglu dynasty. Thank you for meeting with us, disciples of Zoe."

"The chair . . . you just . . . appeared. You're not a ghost, are you?" Zero asked, stunned.

Mrs. Turkoglu turned and looked at Mr. Jenkins, who nodded slowly.

"No, but I have lived for millennia, and I will continue to roam the galaxy until I have righted a mistake I made. Only then will my soul cross into the afterlife. In this matter, I require your assistance.

"It involves an ancient artifact called the Mask of the Shaman King, an object of incredible power that used to belong to my people. It was taken from us and hidden by a secret organization. I contacted Zoe Sitso and she agreed to help us locate it."

"It is our belief that Zoe managed to discover where the Mask was being kept, and so she set up her Nka so that the first clue would be sent to her disciples. The disciples would then be tasked with finding the Mask," said Mr. Jenkins.

"The Mask of the Shaman King is the only thing that can give me peace. Find it and return it to my family. That is the request I have for you, disciples of Zoe. To complete Zoe's Nka," said Mrs. Turkoglu.

She exchanged a loaded glance with Mr. Jenkins.

"There is something else you should know, too. The Mask's power is in distorting reality. And anything that can distort reality can affect the Oblong Dimension," said Mrs. Turkoglu.

There was a sharp intake of breath.

"Zomon," Camih whispered.

Mrs. Turkoglu nodded.

Mr. Gauche's screen face began to show images of roiling storm clouds with lightning bolts forking down toward a dark landscape.

"Thanks to the courage of the Zodiac Sabas, Zomon was banished to the prison realm, condemned to wander for all eternity. But the Mask can be used to weaken the borders between dimensions."

The words fell in the room like a guillotine.

If they failed to find the Mask of the Shaman King and it fell into the wrong hands, then the Dark King responsible for millions of deaths could return.

"Ms. Sitso has left a clue regarding the location of the Mask of the Shaman King," said Mr. Jenkins.

He reached once more inside the chest and pulled out a metal object the size and shape of a cigar, then gave it to Zero.

It felt cool in his palm.

Zero looked at Camih and she stepped closer to look at it.

"What is this?" he asked.

"I think it is a projector," Camih replied.

She took it from him and aimed it at an empty section of wall, twisting the end of it.

A beam of blue light flickered on, and a message, written in cursive, appeared on the wall:

Odunsi Flamengo Nbadu Crescent 4525 R5 3 days

CHAPTER 11

THE whole room was silent.

"Mr. Jenkins, how many people have gotten this exact message besides us?" asked Camih.

Mr. Jenkins slowly locked the chest on the table before turning back to them.

"I am not at liberty to say, madam. I know of at least two others. I was given the task of relaying this information to you two. Others from my law firm will have been sent to meet Zoe's remaining disciples."

"I see," said Zero.

Mr. Jenkins nodded.

"Do you have any more questions for Mr. Jenkins?" asked Mr. Gauche.

Zero and Camih stared at each other.

"No, I think that will do for now," replied Camih.

Mr. Jenkins nodded. He picked up the golden chest and held his arm out to Mrs. Turkoglu. She rose from her seat and bowed her head at them.

"Good luck," she said before she and Mr. Jenkins swept out of the room, leaving Zero, Camih, and Mr. Gauche alone.

"We need to find Ladi. Now," Camih said to Zero after a moment.

Zero nodded. They thanked Mr. Gauche, and Zero followed Camih out of the room, his head crowded with thoughts.

On their way to find Ladi, Camih muttered under her breath.

Zero was a mass of conflicting emotions. On the one hand, he felt special, a member of a select group of people whom Zoe had considered important enough to include in her Nka. On the other hand, Zero also felt pressure. This would be his first mission. What if they failed to find the Mask of the Shaman King? The entire galaxy was at stake.

They stopped in front of the oak double doors near the dorms. A plaque with an electronic display announced in bright blue letters that they had reached the guild's game room.

Inside, they found themselves in a room covered in filigree-patterned wallpaper. Ladi and Octave were sitting on a burgundy couch playing a hologame.

Loud Amapiano music blared from speakers in the corners of the room. Octave was furiously running his thumb in circles around the pad of his controller, while Ladi had his tongue poking out in concentration.

Between the wall and their couch, three holograms were locked in a terrible fighting match.

Camih looked on disapprovingly.

"These boys! All they do is play Saba Warriors 5."

Zero had never seen video games with holograms before. He recognized one of the holograms battling as Zoe. He marveled at the details and the realistic sound effects. Though Camih apparently did not look favorably on video games, Zero wished he could have been playing with the other boys.

"Which one of you is Zoe?" asked Zero.

"That would be Kodjo Teteh from the Titanhearts guild," Octave answered. "I'm Frederick the tenth Capricorn Saba, and Ladi is Gono, the first Jupiter user."

Zero stood up straighter.

Camih looped around the couch and stood in front of the projector on the glass table.

"Ladi, we have important news."

"What?" Ladi asked, craning his neck to look around Camih. His character was now holding Octave's character in a headlock.

Camih reached out and turned off the projector. The three holograms winked out of existence. The boys cried out in horror.

"What did you do that for?" screamed Octave. "We were finally beating Kodjo for the first time in fifty-three games!"

"You'll have other chances, Octave. Right now, we have something we need to discuss with Ladi. Could you leave us for a moment?" said Camih.

Octave got up and sulked out of the room.

Zero and Camih sat down on the couch opposite Ladi.

"Do you have any ongoing missions?" Camih asked him.

"Princess Millina IV of the planet Monfrit has lost her pet poodle. Then the sultan of the planet Kikobo wants flowers and a love letter sent to the djinn singer Cleo. Not looking forward to that because it will involve going through the dragon-infested Destrio asteroid belt. And the Neo Dakar government has commissioned me to explore some ancient Zotorian ruins not too far from here."

"Drop those missions," Camih said. "I have something more interesting for you. Zero, do you want to fill him in?"

Zero told Ladi all about the visit from the lawyer and the Mask of the Shaman King.

When he had finished, Ladi let out a long whistle. He leaned back against the couch, shaking his head in disbelief.

"I know where we can begin looking," he said at last, standing up.

Camih and Zero looked at each other with wide eyes, then followed Ladi out of the room. He led them to the library.

They all settled in at one of the long study tables.

"*Koba-Rekipernix,*" Ladi whispered, and a square-shaped Kobasticker with a red border appeared in front of him. It contained a picture of a black pouch with white wings within a yellow circle. Ladi plucked it from the air and placed it on his forearm.

He then shut his eyes, seeming to concentrate on something. Suddenly, a massive tome appeared and *thunked* onto the table. Zero and Camih leaned in to have a closer look.

Legendary Koba-Objects: The Incredible History of the Mask of the Shaman King by Trevor Noussisi.

"The Mask of the Shaman King is a famous artifact," Ladi murmured. "It is said to be able to alter reality and grant wishes. It was first found among a tribe living on the planet Akatsa."

"The planet where people first made Kobastickers," said Zero.

Ladi nodded.

"The art of making Kobastickers was said to be at its highest point when men first populated Akatsa. It was a golden age. Akatsa was filled with extraordinary Sabas, and all manner of incredible Kobastickers were made using magic from all over the galaxy. The planet was ruled by King Brabus."

Ladi skimmed the book, finding an image of a gaunt old man with eyes like a furnace. He was dressed in a brown cloak and had a long, braided silver beard that fell down to his feet like snow.

"But then tragedy struck. One day King Brabus lost his only son. The king was inconsolable. He wept for fourteen days and fourteen nights. The queen was so distraught that she took her own life. Then, a terrible idea began to take root in the king's mind: He would bring his son back from the dead.

"Among the many clans that lived on Akatsa, there was a secretive clan called the Namakou, who were said to have the secret to a magical mask that could grant wishes. But the Namakou never shared with outsiders their knowledge of how to materialize the Mask. The Namakou were a hardworking and quiet people. They were careful not to draw attention to themselves. If people learned their secret, they would become easy targets for the ambitious and the greedy. But at the time of the king's grief, the Namakou chief was a brash young man eager to advance his station and that of his people. In exchange for riches, the Namakou chief told King Brabus how to materialize the Mask: If he wanted to resurrect the prince, he would have to sacrifice the person who loved the boy the most."

"I'm not sure I understand," said Zero.

"Legend has it that the Mask can grant a single wish, but at great cost. To use the Mask, one must feed it souls, and each time the Mask is used, the number of souls needed to make it work increases. Once a wish is granted, the Mask becomes powerless until twelve years on the planet Akatsa have elapsed. One year on Akatsa equals five months for us, so . . ."

"Five years," finished Zero. "So the king sacrificed himself? But then he would not get to see his son."

Ladi shook his head. "The king was not the person who loved his son the most. He knew that. So he searched his kingdom, killing those who had been close to his son, hoping each time that it would wake the Mask. It was neither the maid who raised the young prince nor his best friend. Instead, it was a young girl the prince had spent his days playing with. She was the niece of the Namakou chief.

"So the king invited the entire Namakou clan to the city for a massive festival to honor their gods. And while the Namakou celebrated, the king kidnapped the chief's niece. Before anyone realized what had happened, it was too late. The clan leaders went to the chief's house to confront him, but when they arrived, he had already taken his own life. He was horrified by what he had done.

"The chief's younger sister—the mother of the sacrificed girl—led a rebellion against the king of Akatsa."

Ladi turned the page of his book to an image of a beautiful woman with a purple Mohawk, blue-tinted skin, and a white horn leading an army of rebels into battle.

"It's her!" cried Zero, looking at Camih. Her eyes were wide.

"You've seen her?" Ladi asked.

"She was the woman we met with today—Selima

Turkoglu," said Camih. "I can't believe she has been roaming the galaxy for this long."

"This woman led the Namakou rebellion. They wanted the king to return the Mask to them. The Namakou could not mourn their princess until the Mask was brought back and a special ritual was carried out so that her soul could be freed. Unfortunately, the Namakou were no match for the king and the rebellion was put down."

"What happened to the king's son?"

Ladi flipped another page of the book. There was a drawing of a procession holding up a small casket.

"He was resurrected. But the king's happiness did not last long. The child was not himself. He was distraught at having been brought back, and eventually he killed himself."

"What happened to the king?"

"Some say he was cursed by the Namakou, and that's why his son killed himself. The king became deeply unpopular and suffered successive waves of rebellions. He fled into exile."

"Mrs. Turkoglu mentioned a secret organization . . ." said Zero, his brow furrowing.

"She was talking about the Order of Lassa, or the Secret Keepers," Ladi explained. "An order of Sabas known to collect ancient and important artifacts. After King Barbus fled, the order recognized the Mask to be dangerous and to attract the worst impulses in man. They stole it from Akatsa before the Namakou could retrieve it."

"And what happened to the Mask after that?" Camih asked.

"Nobody knows."

Ladi shut the book with a meaty slap and threw it casually over his shoulder. It disappeared with a small pop.

"The Order of Lassa died out a hundred years ago, and with it all hope of ever finding the Mask of the Shaman King. That is, until Zoe came along. Finding it won't be easy, though. Countless Sabas have tried and failed to locate it," said Ladi.

"We've got to try nonetheless," said Zero.

Zero was touched by Selima Turkoglu's plight. How could he not be? A mother whose ghost had traveled across millennia to be reunited with an object that contained fragments of her child's soul. Zero felt affection and hope flare inside him. A mother's love could be true.

"Zoe placed her trust in us," he continued. "That's why she addressed the Nka to us."

"And then there is the matter of Zomon," Camih added.

A silence fell over them. For a moment the room seemed to go darker, as if a cloud had passed over the sun.

"Using the Mask would undoubtedly weaken the barrier between the Oblong Dimension and our world. Zomon could break out of his prison and continue his quest to enslave the whole universe. We can't let that happen. We have to return the Mask to Selima," said Camih determinedly.

"I'm in," said Ladi. "I'm hyped. Guild father, mother, and son on a quest to find a magical artifact!"

"But what about Zoe's clue?" asked Zero.

"What about it?" asked Ladi.

"Do we even know what we're looking for?"

Ladi looked at Camih and grinned.

"Oh, that's easy," said Camih.

When Zero continued to look at her blankly, she recited the clue.

"Odunsi Flamengo Nbadu Crescent 4525 R5 3 days. The first part is the address of a branch of the Flamengo Hotel that caters specifically to Sabas. R5 is the number of the room we are to rent for three days."

CHAPTER 12

THE departure date for their first mission together was set. Since this was Zero's first time leaving the guild, he was treated to a Shango Heart tradition: good-luck presents. He got a lot of letters from the other Sabins. He got a knitted scarf from Mr. Gauche. Biscotte dropped a space mammoth bone tied with a red ribbon in front of his door. Halima got him some Musa's Magic Chameleon Shoe Paint, which would allow his Abalo 12s to change color depending on his surroundings. Octave even gave him a signed copy of his latest poem, "Musings of a Bulgoxian Dragon Trapped in a Black Hole." He offered to do a live recital of the poem, but Zero threatened to bite him in the neck, so he dropped the idea.

The day of their departure, Mr. Gauche called for Zero, Ladi, and Camih in the guild meeting room.

When Zero arrived, Mr. Gauche, Ladi, and Camih were already deep in conversation.

Mr. Gauche cleared his throat.

"Zero! I'm glad you could make it. I was just going over a few things with Ladi and Camih, and I wanted to take a moment to talk about your Kobasticker."

Zero looked between them, then shrugged.

"Sure, what about it?" asked Zero.

"As you may know, the moment your identity is revealed as the twenty-fifth user of Jupiter, a lot of people will believe that by killing you, they will be able to become the next wielders of Jupiter and therefore gain immortality."

Zero frowned. "Yes . . . ?" He let the word trail off into a question, unsure where this was going.

"We'd like to push back that moment as far as possible. We want you to make us a promise," said Mr. Gauche.

"We want you to swear you won't use Jupiter in public or tell anyone you possess it," continued Camih.

"But then how am I meant to help you or get better at using it?" complained Zero.

"Right now, our priority is to keep you safe, and that means making sure no one knows that you have Jupiter," said Mr. Gauche. "For that reason, you are not to use Jupiter unless I give you my express permission. Deal?"

"Yes, sir . . ." said Zero reluctantly.

"That was the first thing we want you to promise . . ." said Camih.

She and Ladi exchanged a meaningful glance.

"Why are you looking at each other like that?" demanded Zero suspiciously.

"Zero, a big part of keeping your identity as the twenty-fifth user a secret will be fooling Koba detectors and other machines that might scan your Koba collection," said Camih. "There's good news and bad news. The good news is that we found a Kobasticker with a very similar Koba signature to Jupiter. That way, you will be able to walk through Koba detectors and scanners without revealing that you have Jupiter. The bad news is . . ."

Camih held out two fingers. There was a small clap and a Kobasticker appeared between her index finger and thumb.

"Oh no," said Zero, stumbling backward. "*Cabbagenix!*" he hissed.

Camih nodded somberly.

Cabbagenix gave its user the ability to turn anything they touched into cabbages. It was widely considered the most embarrassing Kobasticker to have in your collection and was consistently ranked the most useless Kobasticker by *Saba Now*. Most Sabas wouldn't be caught dead with Cabbagenix in their possession.

"There has to be another way."

"I'm afraid not."

Ladi was trying hard not to laugh, but looked like he was sitting on a hot pan, doing his best not to shout.

"I had a chat with Halima, and she thinks it is the best course of action. Cabbagenix has the same Koba signature as Jupiter, so if anyone is suspicious you just have to show them Cabbagenix. We figure they'll laugh so hard they'll forget to press you further," said Camih.

"Zero, remember that there are a lot of people who believe that by killing you they will be able to become immortal," said Mr. Gauche.

"I think I'd rather take my chances fighting off people who want to kill me," said Zero, but he nonetheless took the Kobasticker Camih handed to him.

"Well, that went well!" said Ladi cheerfully when they'd

left the room. He was wiping tears of laughter from his eyelashes with his index finger.

"Let's get this party started, guys. We're already behind schedule," said Camih.

"Yes, boss!" Ladi grinned.

As much as Zero would have loved the opportunity to get closer to Camih, he couldn't deny feeling excited that Ladi was joining them. His knowledge of the Mask of the Shaman King would prove invaluable, and his mechanical skills would prove useful. And with the *Ladybug* still out of commission, it was Ladi's whizzer that they would take to the planet Odunsi.

Ladi's was an old whizzer called the *SW Bulldog*. The body looked vaguely like a bulldog's head, and its wings looked like ballet slippers. The entire ship was plastered with thousands of stickers. Ladi couldn't have been more proud of it.

Ladi came from wealth and could no doubt have bought a more recent whizzer model, but he did not get along with his family and he refused on principle to use their money. He funded his whizzer himself doing odd jobs.

According to him, every single part of the *Bulldog* had been replaced at least once. The whizzer was held together by a great deal of industrial-strength duct tape and sheer will.

But it got the job done, and provided you didn't talk above ten decibels or move during the trip, it would take you wherever you needed to go.

Ladi had customized his whizzer with a special hibiscus juice dispenser from Kwaku & Kwaku's and a slime-thrower he had installed to deal with obnoxious whizzer pilots.

The trip to Odunsi was rather uneventful. They stopped

only at a routine police checkpoint where a member of the Space Force examined their papers.

Eventually Ladi shouted, "Buckle up! We are approaching Odunsi!"

Zero stared out the window. A small planet of purple and brown hues could be seen in the distance.

They broke through the planet's atmosphere and headed toward the capital city, which incidentally was also called Odunsi.

It was a market day in Odunsi, and Sabas and non-Sabas alike were walking around the cobbled streets looking for good deals. Ladi landed the *Bulldog* in a whizzer lot close to Nbadu Crescent, the Flamengo Hotel's street.

As they made their way toward the hotel, Zero took in the wooden market stalls brimming with rare fruits, colorful cloth, and strange artifacts. The smell of fried meats wafted to him in the soft breeze, and the chatter of customers haggling with sellers filled the air.

The trio stopped at an intersection barrier to wait for a streetcar packed with people to go by.

The streets were bustling, and as Zero looked around at the crowds, he marveled at the city's diversity. There were elves, fairies, and even a few trolls, as well as countless other alien races dressed in colorful attire.

"I've never seen so many different people before," said Zero.

Ladi nodded. "Odunsi is a big trading city and a very popular tourist destination, so you get people from all over the galaxy here."

As they walked, Ladi pointed out different groups and explained a little bit about them.

"That's a Nillabon," said Ladi, pointing at a rather large creature with wrinkled gray skin, a beaked mouth, and large yellow tusks. "They're a proud warrior race from the planet Neptune 4. Oh, and those are Momoturi, from the planet Momovan."

He pointed at a group of pale creatures in flowing turquoise robes with rather large heads. "Always be careful with them, they can read minds," he whispered.

Zero nodded, then felt something tug at his pants.

A child with bright eyes, freckles, and red hair looked up at Zero and smiled.

Zero smiled back.

"Mister, are you a Saba?" he asked, pointing at the Shango Heart emblem on Zero's shoulder.

Zero nodded. "I am."

The boy gasped.

"Wow! I knew it—"

"Pedro!" A lady dressed in burgundy robes and an elaborate hat strode over to them. The grocery bags she was holding drummed against the side of her hips.

"What did I tell you about wandering off?" She yanked the boy by the wrist. "Come on!"

"Mom, Mom . . . The gentleman has a Saba emblem!"

The lady looked up at Zero, Camih, and Ladi with such malevolence and distrust in her gaze that Zero felt as if he'd been struck in the face.

"Sabas are dangerous criminals, Pedro. Don't let me catch you addressing one again!"

"But Mom—!"

"Quiet!" she shouted, and lugged the boy away. The sound of their quarrel faded as they walked farther down the street.

"You'll get used to it, bud."

Zero turned to Ladi.

"Unfortunately, not everybody is a fan of what we do."

They passed a bounty hunter office, and Zero saw several shady men emerge holding large resin sacks over their shoulders, presumably filled with the money they had received trading in captured people.

On the other side of the street, under a banner that read "Rokimi & Sons," a salesman with oily eyes and a pencil mustache had drawn a sizable crowd in front of his shop.

"Buy these special, limited-edition defensive Kobastickers that will protect you against gunfire, dragon fire, and magic spells! Guaranteed. One hundred percent coverage or your money back. Allow me to demonstrate."

The salesman called out for a volunteer, and a young man dressed in the latest fashions stepped forward. The salesman thrust what looked like a very large laser gun into the volunteer's hands and instructed him to fire.

Zero's gaze swept away from the crowd and fastened on a figure that had been hovering next to a lamppost at the edge of his vision. He locked eyes with a girl with long black hair. She wore black robes and brown shoes, and the bottom half of her face was hidden by a scarf.

He stiffened.

"Zero, you okay?" asked Camih.

Suddenly there was a loud explosion. Zero turned back to the crowd. There was now a salesman-shaped hole in the shopwindow of Rokimi & Sons. Employees came bursting out of the shop with their hair on fire and their arms waving about in the air.

The volunteer slowly lowered the weapon onto the ground and backed away before running full pelt down the road.

Zero turned back to look at the girl, but she was gone.

⬩ 🪁 ⬩ 🐙 ⬩ 🦀 ⬩ 👨‍🚀 ⬩ ✋ ⬩ 🍲 ⬩ 🏚 ⬩ 🎋 ⬩ 🎎 ⬩ 🖐 ⬩ 🐿 ⬩ 🔺 ⬩

The Flamengo Hotel was located in the swanky part of Nbadu Crescent. It was a tall building with a black glass façade. As they approached the front entrance, two burly trolls wearing suits and white earpieces asked them to provide their Saba identification.

They were shown into a luxurious lobby. The ceilings were tall enough that you could have fit five whizzers one on top of the other in the space. There were Sabas wearing colorful-patterned clothes and robes and alien creatures Zero had never seen before. The floors were made of a dark marble, yet Zero could see giant fluorescent fish swimming under their feet.

A few hotel employees wearing crisp black suits and gloves stood watch, and as Zero and his friends walked in, one approached them.

"Welcome, welcome to the Oasis Lounge. How can I help you?"

"We would like a room for three days," said Ladi as the employee guided them to the check-in desk.

"We are actually interested in a particular room," Camih added. "Is Room 5 available?"

"I'm afraid Room 5 is already taken."

Zero felt his heart sink.

"It has been booked for a month. But we have a number of other rooms available."

"What about 15? Or 25?" Camih asked, urgently. "It may sound ridiculous, but we have a superstition, see. We won't go into a room unless it has the number five at the end."

The concierge shook his head. "I'm sorry, madam. It so happens that all the rooms with the number five have been taken. A young woman booked them just this morning, actually."

"All the rooms containing the number five?" Ladi asked incredulously.

"Yes, sir. All eleven rooms. From Rooms 5 to 55. You can see for yourselves," said the concierge, turning the screen toward them.

Ladi and Camih stared at each other.

"Someone else is looking for the—" Ladi began.

"Shh," Camih hissed before he could say more.

"What about Room 7?" Zero asked suddenly.

Camih and Ladi looked at him, confusion plain on their faces.

The concierge looked down at a screen.

"Room 7 is available. It was vacated just this morning, actually."

"Then we'll take that one. For three days," said Zero.

Camih raised an eyebrow at him. "I hope you know what you're doing."

"Trust me," said Zero. "I'll explain later."

Camih reached for something in her pocket and took out a single gold coin. She handed the oath to the concierge.

The concierge dropped the coin inside a slot on the desk, listening to it slide down the chute. The next moment, a key popped out of a slot, carved in the shape of a python. The concierge slid the key across the marble counter. Zero took it just as a voice behind him said:

"Camih, is that you? And Ladi, you too?"

A young man had silently appeared beside them. He wore slippers, what looked like bright red swim trunks with palm trees drawn on them, and a trench coat. He had his blond hair in a bob, and a smile you could power a small planet with.

"Uncle Conor?" Camih gasped.

"How do you do?"

"What are you doing here?" she cried, excitement rising in her voice.

"Just finished a consultancy for the Intergalactic Fairy Bank. Now I'm taking a break before taking on more guild activity. Who is your new friend?" he asked, turning to Zero.

Zero was still observing this stranger with an affable exterior and blasé attitude, but mainly he was trying to figure out why Ladi was looking at him like a puppy staring at the femur of a very large dinosaur.

"This is Zero, a Sabin," Camih explained. "He joined the guild recently. Zero, this is Conor Reed. He is also a member of Shango Heart."

Mr. Reed reached out and shook Zero's hand.

"I think Mr. Gauche might have mentioned you. It's a pleasure meeting you, Zero." He adjusted his trench coat. "Anyway, I'm about to go do some sightseeing. I expect we'll bump into each other again."

And with that, Mr. Reed turned and walked out of the lobby.

The trio made their way toward the elevator banks.

"Well, if it isn't the pipsqueaks from Shango Guild!" cried a voice.

Zero turned around.

A tall boy with a sharp nose, olive skin, and short black hair was smirking at them. He looked like the type of person who relishes other people's downfall. He was flanked by a gang of boys wearing enough leather to make old ladies cross the street.

"Khabib," Camih gritted out, as if she were addressing something smelly that had stuck to her foot.

"In the flesh."

Zero was staring at the guild emblem on Khabib's collar. Where had he seen it before . . . ?

"The Scorpiodukes," said Zero, remembering. He had heard of them. They were a very recent guild that specialized in bounty hunting. They were quickly rising through the guild rankings.

"It's been a long time," said Khabib.

"Not long enough, as far as I'm concerned," growled Ladi.

"I second that," added Camih.

"You're hurting my feelings," said Khabib sarcastically. "What are you doing here?"

"We're on a mission," Camih answered bluntly. "What are you doing here?"

"We're on a *special* mission. We're Sabas now. The whole gang. Mama Dabi registered the guild."

"You're space bandits. You kidnap people for money," said Camih.

"Not anymore. We're on the straight and narrow. Being a Saba is where it's at now. Mama Dabi wonders why we didn't think of it before."

"I can't believe the Saba Organization would give you guys a license," said Ladi, shaking his head.

"Well, they did," Khabib snarled.

He turned to Camih. "I bet you regret leaving Mama Dabi now, but it's too late. She's completely forgotten about you. Barely even mentions you."

"That's right," said one of Khabib's minions.

"Barely," parroted another.

Camih gripped Zero's and Ladi's arms and turned back toward the elevators. "Let's go, guys," she mumbled.

CHAPTER 13

THEIR room was on the second floor, and it had a view of the rose-colored sea. In the distance, thunderclouds were forming a dark band occasionally cut by forks of lightning.

As soon as they got inside their room, Camih rounded on Zero.

"Now can you tell us why we're in this room? I'm not sure I understand," said Camih.

"The code. I think we might have misinterpreted it. *Odunsi Flamengo Nbadu Crescent 4525 R5 3 days*. It's an address, so we assumed R5 was just the room number. But R5 was Zoe's favorite boy band."

"We know. That's why we thought she would have chosen Room 5."

"Right. But I don't think that's what R5 means. It could be referring to another room number. The word for 'musicians' in Ewodo, the ancient Africana language, is *amévé*. Ewodo, like most ancient languages that came from Africana, is based on intonations and context. In some instances, *amévé* can also mean 'seven.' Zoe loved to play games like this, and she loved Africana culture."

Ladi whistled, impressed. "Should we search the room?" he asked.

Camih nodded and together they rummaged around the room. They looked in the drawers, under the bed, and in the bathroom cupboards. But after a good thirty-five minutes, they all met back in the living room.

"Found anything?" asked Camih.

Zero and Ladi shook their heads.

Zero felt a prickle of anxiety. Perhaps he had gotten it all wrong? And yet the clue seemed to ring so true. He was convinced that the logic that had led him to Room 7 was the exact logic Zoe would use. They were in the right room, but they weren't looking in the right place.

"Maybe whatever the next clue is isn't in the room," Zero mused. "Maybe it will be delivered to this room. Maybe that's why the instructions tell us to book the room for three days!" He was eager to latch onto anything that would distract from the fact that they might not be in the right room.

"I hadn't thought of that," said Camih. "We should take turns standing watch. That way, there will always be one of us in the room in case someone comes in. How does that sound?"

Zero and Ladi nodded their agreement.

Camih turned to Zero. "Why don't you check out one of the vending machines and buy yourself a Kobasticker? I know buying my first Kobasticker was a big deal! I'll stay here. I'm pretty tired."

"So am I," said Ladi. "I feel like I could sleep for days."

Camih handed Zero a few oaths. Zero thanked her and headed out, disappointed that Camih had chosen to stay behind rather than explore the hotel with him.

The hallways were plush and grandiose, with beautiful handcrafted burgundy carpets and wood-paneled walls. He passed groups of Sabas who were talking in languages he had never heard before.

As Zero walked through the halls of his hotel, his attention was caught by voices up ahead, coming from beyond the Kobasticker vending machine.

"What did they look like?" asked a deep, gruff voice that sounded exactly like Zero imagined an evil henchman would sound.

"There was a tall boy with blue hair and a boy with an X-shaped scar on his cheek and a blue bandanna around his neck. Then there was a tall girl, pretty, with dreadlocks. She looked familiar. I think she's some big-shot young Saba," replied a voice that was younger and nasal.

Zero froze in his tracks.

"They were asking a lot of questions about rooms containing the number five."

"You think they're after the Mask too?

"Must be."

Zero felt a spool of fear uncoil in his stomach. There was no one else in the corridor, but the two men's shadows extended from beyond the vending machine. If they so much as poked their heads out from around the vending machine, they would see him.

Zero moved closer to the vending machine so he could no longer be seen. He was breathing quickly and the metal was hot against his back.

"Should we tell the boss?" asked the second voice.

"No. We keep monitoring them. We need to know

everything they are doing before we report back. Keep an eye out and let me know their next steps. I need to head back to my room."

Zero's breath caught in his throat. If they walked in his direction, they would find Zero hiding in the shadows and would know immediately that he had been spying on them.

He heard the man walking toward him, saw his shadow lengthen over the carpet.

The shadow froze. A ringed finger flashed across the corner of the vending machine.

There was a hissing sound.

"I forgot my key in the lobby," groaned the first voice.

"I'll come with you," said the second voice.

The sound of footsteps retreated from the vending machine.

Zero breathed a sigh of relief.

But almost immediately he realized that he had missed an opportunity to see who had been speaking. He peered around the machine, but they were gone. He was alone, standing in the electronic green glow of the vending machine.

Zero stared at the Kobastickers on sale in front of him. There were all shapes and sizes. Next to each of them were small screens describing their abilities and their names.

Zero rubbed the oaths Camih had given him together in his pocket. The Kobastickers in the vending machine were quite expensive. There wasn't much he could afford. He hesitated between one called Steaknix, which made anything you ate taste like a juicy camel steak (there was just one left), and one called Puddlenix. According to the description, it allowed the user to materialize puddles, which he could then freely control.

Zero decided to go for that one. He slipped two oaths into the coin slot and pressed the button. An arrow appeared on the screen pointing to a cavity just above the coin slot. The words *Your Kobasticker is ready, please place your hand in the stamping area* were below it.

Zero placed his hand in the cavity palm-down. He was startled when he felt something wet and cool stamp onto the back of his hand.

Zero pulled out his hand and looked at his new Kobasticker, its outlines glowing with a bright blue light. It winked a few times on the back of his hand and then disappeared.

"Z-zero?" stuttered a voice behind him.

How stupid could he have been? Perhaps the two men had returned!

Zero whirled around and found himself face-to-face with the girl he had seen at the market.

"Efua? What are you doing here?"

She wore a black beret over her long black hair, and her almond-shaped green eyes were pretty but inscrutable, shielding the thoughts hiding behind them. Her young face was hard, like someone who had grown up a lot in a short space of time.

"I could be asking you the same thing!" she said brightly.

At the sight of her, it was as if the years melted away and he was once more in Cégolim. Efua had spent most of her time rebelling against Jude's authority and dreaming about joining her favorite Saba guild, Lionheart. She had been one of the two people to have been banished from Cégolim, after Jude accused her of being a witch.

On her last night in the city, Zero had been in his room putting up a new R5 poster when there was a knock on his door. He'd opened it to find Efua beaming at him. Her eyes had been as bright as fireworks.

"Zero, how do you do? Can I come in?"

Zero had been confused as to why she was there, but he'd let her in. All he'd really known of Efua was that she did not get along with her cousin Jude.

"Is that an R5 poster? Very nice!" She'd pointed to the poster he had just put up.

Zero had felt respect for her kindling inside him. It had been nice having his taste in music validated by a popular girl like Efua.

"I don't want to take too much of your time right now," she'd begun, "I know we have not spoken much, but tomorrow I will be challenging Jude to a fight that will determine who is the ruler of Cégolim. I trust you know Jude is not fit to be the ruler of Cégolim—he would terrorize everyone who lives here and turn this city into a living hell. I have gathered a group of children who are just as concerned as I am and who will be fighting with me. I would be honored if you would join us in defeating that little sleazeball."

She'd curled her fingers into fists for emphasis.

"We will be meeting at nine a.m. near the Tree of Bob. If you would like to be a part of history, then meet me there! Can I count on you?"

"Sure," Zero had said, shrugging.

Efua had nodded. She'd patted Zero on the shoulder, thanked him, and left.

Of course, Zero had overslept the next day and come late to the meeting spot. By the time he'd arrived, he learned Efua's fate: None of the people she had recruited had shown up. She alone had gone to challenge Jude. She was defeated and banished from the city.

Zero had always felt ashamed by what had happened. He'd wondered if things would have turned out differently if he had been there to help her. And he wondered if she resented him.

As he looked at her now, he felt that all her excitement and energy was gone. Even her smile seemed like a pale imitation of the warmth she'd radiated before. He wondered just what things had happened to her to make her lose all that.

"It's great seeing you again," said Efua.

"Likewise. It's been a really long time."

"I know, right? It seems we've both become Sabas! What are the odds? What guild did you join?"

"Shango Heart," replied Zero carefully.

"Oh wow! You joined a pretty famous guild," she said.

"And what about you? How is Lionheart?"

For a moment the happiness on her face faltered and a shadow of shame crept through. She rubbed her thumb and index finger together as though she were sprinkling a handful of invisible salt.

"I didn't join Lionheart. I joined the Viperkings, not sure if you've heard of them . . . ?" she asked, her voice trailing off.

"Of course I've heard of them. They're full of very popular

Sabas!" Zero shook his head, smiling. "You haven't changed. Always doing incredible things."

"I know you're trying to cheer me up, so thank you." Efua smiled softly. "What brings you to Odunsi?"

Zero hesitated. Though he knew Efua, he felt cagey about their mission.

"We're on a hunt for a rare object," he hedged.

"*We're*? Some members of your guild are here too?"

Zero nodded.

"We came here looking for a room with the number five in it—"

"I owe you an apology then."

Zero blinked, realization dawning on him. "You're the one who booked all those rooms?"

"Yes. I guess you received an Nka from Zoe too?"

Zero's jaw dropped.

"I guess we do have quite a lot of catching up to do," Efua sighed. "I knew Zoe too, after I left Cégolim."

She reached inside her coat and pulled out a gold medallion. Zero recognized it immediately—Zoe had given him an identical one.

Efua changed the subject. "You mentioned you were with some friends of yours . . ."

Zero nodded.

"They're part of Shango Heart too."

An idea popped into Zero's head.

"Would you like to meet them?"

Efua seemed to consider this.

"I wouldn't want to disturb—" she began.

"I'm sure they would be glad to meet you."

Efua nodded her head. "All right then."

When Zero and Efua got to the suite, Ladi and Camih were sitting at the dining table staring at hologram screens. Camih was checking the prices on a range of new whizzers, and Ladi was answering fan mail on his Sigmia account.

Camih turned off her screen as they entered the room.

"Hey guys, this is my friend Efua. I bumped into her at the Kobasticker vending machine down the corridor. She used to live in Cégolim too."

"Hi! I'm Camih Sitso, and this is Ladi Hyung," said Camih, gesturing to Ladi, who waved.

"Pleased to meet you. I suppose I should start with this," said Efua.

She reached inside her coat and pulled out Zoe's medallion.

Instinctively Zero reached for his own medallion around his neck, his fingers tracing its shape. Camih did the same. Their medallions were identical.

"I was friends with Zoe once. The other day, a fellow from Jenkins & Jenkins & Jenkins visited me to give me her Nka."

Zero thought about Zoe and her influence on his life, and then imagined all the lives she had touched with her enthusiasm and energy. He felt something tremble in his gut. But it wasn't all bad. For the first time, he realized that each person in the room had unique memories of Zoe and had seen sides of her that Zero had never known.

"I've been trying to solve Zoe's Nka, but unfortunately

I've spent a small fortune and have very little to show for it," said Efua.

"Are you the one who booked all the rooms?" Ladi asked Efua.

"I'm afraid so," said Efua. "I was thinking we could collaborate. We can share our information and work as a team to find the Mask of the Shaman King. Zoe would have wanted that."

Zero looked at Camih.

"Could I have a word with you two?" Camih asked him and Ladi. She got to her feet.

"Take your time," said Efua, nodding.

"Thank you," said Camih.

Zero and Ladi followed her into the adjoining room and shut the door.

"What do you guys think?" Camih asked them quietly.

"It can't hurt to pool our resources," Ladi mused. "Besides, she's booked all the rooms ending in five. If a clue does turn up in one of her rooms, then she will be obligated to let us know. What do you think, bud?" Ladi asked Zero.

"It makes sense, I guess," said Zero slowly. "And she has Zoe's medallion."

"Do you trust her?" asked Camih.

Zero thought for a moment. "I haven't seen her in a long time . . ." he began uncertainly. "But yes, I trust her."

Camih nodded. "All right. Then I say we work with her. Agreed?"

Zero and Ladi nodded.

"There's something else," said Zero.

He told them about the strange conversation he had overheard in the corridor.

"We shouldn't be surprised. A lot of people want the Mask of the Shaman King. We need to be very careful from this point onward," said Ladi.

They returned to the room, and Efua was waiting for them in a chair.

"We'll work with you," said Camih. "I'll add you on Sigmia, and Zero will let you know if we find anything."

"That would be perfect," said Efua. "I'll be in Room 5 for now."

When she was gone, they all sat down on the living room couches.

"Why didn't you tell us that you knew a beautiful girl like that?" asked Ladi, elbowing Zero in the ribs.

Zero blushed, avoiding Camih's gaze.

"At any rate," Camih said, "I figure we need all the help we can get. I certainly believe that Zoe would have wanted us to work together."

Zero was about to agree when a knock sounded at the door.

CHAPTER 14

ZERO and Camih exchanged glances.

"Maybe she forgot something?" offered Ladi.

"I'll go check," said Zero.

He got to his feet and went to the door, but when he opened it, there was no one there.

Zero shrugged. He was about to turn around when he noticed a brown envelope lying across the threshold.

Zero poked his head outside and looked down both sides of the corridor. It was empty.

"Who was it?" asked Camih.

"Not sure, but they left this." Zero held up the envelope as he shut the door and walked back toward them.

"You think it might be the next clue?" asked Ladi.

"Open it," said Camih.

Inside the envelope on a folded piece of paper was written a single line:

Be careful. You are being watched. Come to Bizquash Street in front of Huarang Bookstore at midnight. There you will find what you seek.

"I don't like this. It could be a trap. What if the two people Zero overheard are behind this?" Ladi.

"I don't think we have a choice," said Zero.

"I agree with you, Zero," said Camih. "We need to call Efua and fill her in."

"So we're going?" Ladi groaned.

"I don't see any other way," said Camih.

Camih called Efua. She seemed to share Ladi's opinion that the meeting could be a trap. If they were to go, she suggested, they shouldn't tell anybody else their plans.

They decided to hunker down in their rooms until eleven to avoid suspicion.

Zero tried to rest after the day's journey, but before he knew it, it was time to go. His anxiety was like a ball of lead in his stomach as they loaded up their backpacks.

They left their rooms and were joined by Efua in the corridor. They decided to sneak out a side entrance rather than leave through the lobby.

They made their way along a cobbled street that bordered the Borix River. The moon was a silvery melt on the surface of the water, and the air was chilly.

The streets were quiet apart from the occasional group heading to or from one of the crowded bars they passed.

Zero and the crew kept darting looks behind their backs as they went. They stuck to dark alleys and walked around the same squares twice to throw anyone following them off their trail.

They arrived at the meeting place at 11:58. The Huarang Bookstore was a small establishment at the end of Bizquash Street that specialized in goblin literature.

The street was deserted, and the crew waited in silence as far from the pale, lemon-colored wash of the nearby streetlight as they could get. Up above, the sky was dappled with thick black clouds.

A wind picked up and sent an old newspaper gliding across the pavement.

"Eyes alert," said Camih.

Zero nodded. His face felt numb from the cold.

After a moment, he heard footsteps.

Camih and Ladi grew still.

"They're getting closer," whispered Efua.

A man appeared next to the lamppost.

"Chuksapanza!" breathed Zero.

The man wore dark robes, a melon hat, and dark shades. But he was trembling, and his face was a deathly pale color like the underside of a mushroom.

When he spoke, his voice was tinged with urgency.

"Are you disciples of Zoe?"

They all nodded. Zero, Camih, and Efua pulled out their medallions.

"We do not have much time ... very dangerous men ... after the Mask ... wish to use its power to cause great harm ..."

As he spoke, Zero noticed a trail of dark liquid that ended where the man stood.

Blood.

The man stumbled. Instinctively, Zero reached out and grabbed him by the arm so he would not fall.

"He's badly hurt," whispered Efua.

Zero heard the low rumble of thunder.

"Please, sir, you came to give us a message. What is it?" coaxed Zero.

But the man was dying. His attention was like a balloon drifting up into the sky.

Zero had a strong urge to shake him, to get his attention to settle, but then Ladi shouted:

"Over there!"

They all turned as one.

On the other side of the street, a solitary figure raised a palm toward them.

There was a loud *bang* followed by a bolt of light that roared toward them.

Zero felt a puff of displaced air as the man he was holding up was sent crashing against the wall behind them.

The figure across the street turned and ran.

Zero started to chase after him, but Camih grabbed him by the arm.

"Don't! It's too dangerous. He could be leading you into an ambush. And this man needs help!"

The injured man was slumped against the wall. His eyes were the size of plates and he clutched his stomach. Smoke rose from his charred clothes and singed skin.

He was breathing heavily, and blood pooled on the sidewalk next to him.

Ladi was by his side in an instant.

"*Koba-Curenix,*" he said.

In a tiny thunderclap, a pill-shaped Kobasticker appeared above Ladi's palm. He plucked the Kobasticker out of the air and pressed it against his forearm. He then grabbed the man by the wrist. Zero watched as blue lines began to spread out from the Kobasticker, down through Ladi's hand, and up the man's arm like cracks. They reached the man's shoulder and began regressing.

"This is not going to be enough. This man needs to see a doctor," said Ladi as the lines faded entirely.

The man coughed, his whole body seizing.

For a moment a light came into his eyes. He reached out to Zero with a trembling fist.

Zero took his hand and felt him press something into his palm. The man's arm went limp as his life seemed to be sucked out of him.

"It's over," Camih whispered.

Zero opened his fist to find a crumpled piece of paper. He was about to unfold it when a blinding light spotlighted them against the wall.

A voice shouted, "Hands up! Get away from the man's body."

"You have got to be joking," groaned Ladi.

"I repeat: Get away from the man!"

Slowly Zero, Camih, Efua, and Ladi stood up, hands raised.

Across the street, a tall woman in a gray trench coat stood flanked by half a dozen Space Force officers. She wore a red visor that covered her eyes. The officers' laser guns were aimed Zero and the others, pinpoints of red light hovering over their chests like fireflies.

"Officer, you're making a mistake—" began Zero.

"Let me be the judge of that. Face the wall."

Slowly they obeyed.

"Officer—" Zero tried again.

"Not another word! You're all under arrest for first-degree murder."

CHAPTER 15

AN icy wind was blowing across the streets, sending trash and leaves gliding down the road. Above them, the streetlamp flickered on and off. Zero's breath escaped in white vapors.

Zero's mind was bustling with activity.

"Get down on your knees," the officer ordered.

"Officer, we don't have anything to do with this! Honestly!" cried Ladi.

"Sure," the woman said sarcastically. "Then come to the station with me and we'll straighten this out."

Zero winced.

"No can do, Officer," said Camih.

"*Excuse me?*" the woman shouted.

"Officer, please listen to us—" Zero began.

"No, *you* are going to listen to *me*. I'm giving you five seconds to get on your knees. Five . . ."

Zero felt a drop of sweat trickle down his cheek. Out of the corner of his eye, he noticed a figure detach itself from the shadows.

Zero recognized Conor Reed's bright red swimming trunks.

Mr. Reed caught Zero's eye and waved.

Zero heard a sharp intake of breath from each of his friends.

"Er . . . Officer . . ." said Zero, trying to face her.

"Turn around," the woman barked. "Three ... two ..."

"One," finished Mr. Reed, his voice ringing out into the night.

The policemen whirled toward Mr. Reed just as he pressed his fingers against the back of his forearm. A Kobasticker began to glow as his eyes filmed over with white.

There was an explosion and a spiral of purple smoke rose up from the ground to engulf the policemen.

Zero pinched his nose and shut his eyes as the cloud of smoke swallowed them.

When he opened his eyes again, the smoke had settled. Mr. Reed stood with a grin on his face. The officers were all strewn around the street.

"Uh-oh," said Zero. "They're not ..." He couldn't voice the word.

Mr. Reed shook his head. "Just passed out. They will wake up soon with nothing but a headache and an appetite like a Plutonian Olephant."

He crouched down and searched the head inspector's pockets. He pulled out a wallet and flipped it open.

Zero, meanwhile, was staring in admiration at Mr. Reed. Apart from Mr. Gauche, he had never seen anyone use a Kobasticker without having to say activation words. He supposed Mr. Reed must be a very advanced Saba.

"Inspector Priya," read Mr. Reed.

"We're in trouble," said Camih.

"That's an understatement," Ladi groaned. "We're fugitives now. And our only lead died before we could get any meaningful information from him!"

"I wouldn't say that," said Zero. He held up the crumpled piece of paper that the informer had passed on to him.

The rest of the company all huddled closer to read it.

"The answer is in the Bluedust SE 1am car 25J," Zero read.

"The *Bluedust*—that's the Saba Express. There must be one that leaves at one a.m.!" cried Camih.

Zero had dreamed about riding Saba's special intergalactic train. He and Camih locked eyes.

"What time is it?" asked Camih.

Zero looked at his Goooober. "Twelve twenty."

"We have forty minutes to get to the station," said Camih.

Inspector Priya began to stir.

"You need to get out of here," said Mr. Reed.

"What about you?" asked Camih worriedly.

"I'll stick around. As an S-Class Saba, I have immunity. By the time they waive it, you'll be far away. I trust you will have sorted out this misunderstanding by then."

Camih looked at Ladi and then at Zero. "He's right. We need to get out of here."

"Quick!" said Mr. Reed as the inspector's hands twitched.

Zero and his friends hurried down the street. Zero cast one last look at the lifeless body of the informer, thanking him silently.

They reached the Saba Express station without stopping once. Zero kept darting looks over his shoulder, expecting to see an army of Space Force officers chasing after them.

The Odunsi train station was teeming with people despite the late hour. The four of them rushed to the main platform, where the Saba Express was stationed. Its polished sides gleamed like a wolf's teeth. A loose crowd of people were standing around the platform, waiting to board. Plumes of blue smoke escaped from the train's chimney and swept over the crowd like a blue tide.

"I'll buy the tickets, you guys wait here," said Ladi. He went over to the ticket offices.

Zero thought of the hateful woman at the market. She would have been ecstatic to see her worst assumptions about Zero realized.

Ladi reappeared with four tickets.

"I managed to get tickets on the J car."

They took the tickets and quickly joined one of the lines of passengers boarding the train. There were at least twelve people in front of them.

It was only a matter of time before Inspector Priya regained her senses. She would immediately send out instructions to arrest the four friends. For all Zero knew, the information was being relayed all across Odunsi as they stood there on the platform, spreading like fire through a dry forest.

There was a shout behind Zero.

Have we been found out already? Zero felt a throb of fear.

He turned around, but it was only someone calling after a friend to hurry up.

Zero looked back toward the line to board the train. It had barely moved. Zero tapped his foot impatiently. At the front of the line, an older female Saba was busy searching in her bag for her license.

"Come on, come on, come on!" Ladi muttered under his breath.

The moment they boarded the train they would be on neutral ground. Safe. But right now, Zero felt like a man stuck out in the open, seeing thunderheads building in the distance.

Zero glanced toward the other end of the platform and felt a stab of panic: two constables were making their way through the crowd toward them. Their eyes scanned the passengers casually. Ladi tapped Camih on the arm to warn her, and she swore under her breath.

There were two people ahead of them now.

Zero looked back toward the officers. For a heartbeat, Zero locked eyes with one of them before he quickly turned back to face the ticketmaster. His cheeks felt hot.

They were finally next in line. He could see the inside of the train, the warm yellow light in the corridors and the passengers reading in their booths, blissfully unaware of the specter of a police arrest.

Zero clenched and unclenched his fists.

"Tickets and Saba licenses, please!" said the ticketmaster, cutting through Zero's thoughts.

The ticketmaster was a walrus-like creature dressed in a blue uniform.

It looked at Camih and Ladi's credentials and let them through.

It did the same for Efua.

Zero was next. He stepped forward and handed over his documents. The ticketmaster looked at his Sabin card, frowning in concentration.

Zero risked one more look toward the approaching constables. His stomach sank. One was standing with a hand to his earpiece, a stony look on his face. He quickly spoke to his colleague, and they began to scan the crowd with a lot more determination.

They know, Zero thought.

The ticketmaster followed his gaze and frowned.

"Is everything okay?" he asked, his eyes creased into slits.

The policemen were jogging through the crowd about thirty feet from Zero, inspecting the faces of passersby.

"Have you finished with my card?" Zero asked, reaching for his ticket.

The ticketmaster hesitated, glancing once more at the policemen.

"Come on, Zero!" Camih said, her voice full of forced cheer. She stood at the car steps and addressed the ticketmaster. "Is there a problem, sir?"

Slowly, the ticketmaster stepped aside, shaking his head. "No, miss."

He handed Zero his card, and Zero slipped into the car just as the policemen reached their line.

Zero felt a wave of relief wash over him.

"That was close," said Zero, eager to put as much distance as possible between them and the policemen.

"Where are we seated?" asked Efua.

Ladi checked the tickets. "22, 23, 24, and 25J," he read.

The inside of the train was luxurious, with wood-paneled walls and thick carpets with intricate patterns. Passengers sat in soft seats in wine-colored cubicles, with mahogany tables on which sat gilded lamps. Beautiful chandeliers dangled from the middle of the ceiling, throwing arrows of light across the walls.

Their car was mercifully empty.

The four seats faced each other next to the window.

"We made it!" said Camih once they'd sat down.

"How long before the train leaves?" asked Zero.

Camih looked at her watch.

"Two minutes. And it looks like we've got company."

Zero froze. Just outside, he saw a familiar figure speaking to a small throng of eager constables.

Inspector Priya.

A whistle pealed loudly as the train lurched into motion.

Quick, quick, quick! Zero begged silently.

For a brief moment, he locked eyes with Inspector Priya. Anger bloomed across her face just as the train hissed forward, a cloud of steam washing over the platform and hiding them from view.

With a tug and a pull, the train climbed into the air, tunneling through the landing rings like a belt being pulled off a pair of pants.

"That was way too close," Zero sighed.

A steward soon arrived, pushing a trolley with hot cocoa, pastries, hibiscus juice, and snacks.

The friends politely declined, and the trolley moved on to another car.

On the car's television screen, Zero recognized a familiar face. He tapped Ladi's arm, and the group turned to watch.

"Benoz Lenoir, the infamous Dark Saba, has been arrested trying to steal crackers from a convenience store on Neptune 4," the newscaster announced.

The Kobasticker hunter looked unrecognizable dressed in a tattered gray hoodie, army camo shorts, and sneakers. Zero watched as he was lugged out of the convenience store in handcuffs by a few policemen before being shoved into a police hover car.

"Well, at least we know he survived the whizzer landing on him," Camih grumbled.

"What do we do now?" asked Efua.

"The clue. We need to search the car for anything that might be related to the Mask," said Zero.

"Perhaps we are waiting for someone, like before?" proposed Efua.

"Maybe. But knowing Zoe, I doubt she would use the same trick twice," said Zero.

The crew began their search of the car. They inspected the windows, the luggage cubbies, and the seats but found nothing. They even leafed through the various magazines on display, and still they found nothing that might be a clue. They found no hidden symbols, no inscriptions, no hidden compartments.

"We have to try to be logical about this. Where would Zoe leave a clue in this car?" said Camih.

"Keeping a clue on a commercial train used by thousands of people? They would have cleaners wiping this place spotless from floor to ceiling every day. They also change the cushions once in a while, which means that almost every space in this car will have been cleaned, replaced, or updated," said Efua.

The solution dropped into Zero's mind.

"The tables," said Zero. "That's one part of the car that rarely changes. They don't have to be replaced as much."

Efua frowned. "We checked them already, there's noth—"

"*Under* the tables."

Without another word, Zero dropped to his knees and peered under the long table in front of him.

He discovered an incredible number of scratches, tally marks, names, and discolored pieces of chewing gum, but nothing that had a link to the Mask of the Shaman King.

"Everyone split up and look underneath the tables."

The friends did as Zero said.

"I think I found something!" said Efua from their table at 25J.

Everyone gathered around her.

"There's some kind of code written under here. A lot of numbers and letters," said Efua.

Zero scrabbled in his backpack for a pen and paper. "Read it out."

Zero wrote down everything Efua said and made her repeat it for extra confirmation.

When she finished, he backed away and looked at what he had written like a painter admiring his work.

GDRK22 503-1530592002

"Anyone know what that means?" asked Zero.

But he noticed Camih and Ladi were looking anxiously at each other.

"There's good news and there's bad news," began Camih.

"The good news is, I know exactly what the message is referring to. It's the number of a vault at Goldrick Bank. Zoe took me there once."

"And the bad part?" Zero pressed.

"Goldrick Bank happens to be owned by the Space Mafia."

CHAPTER 16

"**WE** have another problem," said Zero. He pointed back to the TV screen at the head of the car.

At that very moment, photographs of Zero, Camih, Ladi, and Efua along with their names were being broadcast on the news.

Ladi let out a groan.

"The Space Force will probably be waiting for us as soon as we get to Goldrick. And even if by some miracle we were able to slip past them, our faces are going to be everywhere. There is no way we can just walk into the bank without being recognized," said Efua.

"What we need are disguises," Camih said. "The Society of the Black Rose."

"You cannot be serious," said Ladi.

"The who-of-the-what now?" asked Zero.

"The Society of the Black Rose is an unlicensed, underground network of merchants selling objects and Saba equipment—some of it legal. It can only be accessed by members—which I happen to be. They only accept their own Dark Saba currency, called crows, which cannot be traced by the Saba Organization."

"But how are you going to get those items here?" asked Zero.

"You'll see," said Camih.

A few minutes later, their car door slid open and another steward pushing a trolley appeared.

"Can I interest you in some spells?" the steward asked. "We have a wide selection of Kobastickers from Mandelson & Sons."

Zero stared at the side of the trolley where a menu showed the Kobastickers on offer and their prices. He noticed a few elemental types like Firenix and Icenix, and quite a few object-summoning Kobastickers.

"Actually, I was wondering if we could have something else," said Camih.

She motioned to the steward with a finger. As the steward leaned in, Camih whispered something in her ear that Zero couldn't hear.

The steward straightened up as if struck by lightning. She looked at Camih, her eyes wide.

"Er . . . why yes, madam . . . If you would give me just a moment . . ."

She turned and ran, leaving them alone with the trolley.

"What did you tell the steward?" asked Zero.

Suddenly the lights in the car flickered and then went out.

A cold gust of wind picked up, making Zero shudder. The windows creaked as white frost bloomed across them like flowers.

A white mist filled the car up to their knees. The chandeliers flickered back on, basking them in a pale blue light.

The wooden trolley was now shiny and black, like onyx. Standing next to it was a bulky goblin with slits for eyes and scaly hands that poked out from under the cuffs of a tattered brown hooded robe.

"You asked for us?" grumbled the creature in a voice like a nest of snakes after it's been disturbed.

Camih walked over to the trolley, searched inside her pocket, and pulled out three silver oaths. There was a mechanical contraption on top of the trolley that looked like a cash register with a handle and a coin slot.

She placed the three coins in the slot and pulled the lever. There was a soft rustle as the tokens slid down a metal chute deep into the machine, and a *clink* as they reached the bottom. A few moments later, a receipt printed on a piece of parchment was produced from an opening at the bottom of the machine. The goblin yanked it out and inspected it.

"You are indeed a member. How can we help you? We have a selection of powerful Dark Kobastickers to suit any purpose you have," said the goblin softly.

Zero noticed that the Kobastickers on display had changed. His gaze fell on a circular one named Abyssfire with a picture of a person being consumed by flames. There was an octagonal Kobasticker called Fenrir with a wolf trampling people armed with spears.

"We need transformation Kobastickers, preferably from the Lupin series, for some disguises."

"I have something better," said the goblin. He smiled, exposing a set of razor-sharp teeth.

Then he pressed a button on the side of the trolley and a panel flipped open, revealing a compartment filled with masks. There were faces of women, men, children, and even trolls. Zero stared at a particularly striking mask of a dark-skinned man with an eye patch. The faces seemed so real . . .

Zero felt a chill. He hoped that these were not the faces of actual people.

He swallowed thickly.

"These are from the Moriarty series. They are the very best transformation Dark Kobastickers money can buy. Each comes with a set of two disguises, male and female. After that, you can copy the appearances of people you know. Undetectable and untraceable. The Kobasticker can be used an unlimited number of times, but the disguises only last two hours, and then you have to wait six hours to use them again. Each Kobasticker comes with voice modifiers, three outfit changes, a detailed biography of the disguises, and a guarantee that covers the first two changes—"

"That's not a lot," said Zero.

"It's the industry standard, sir," replied the goblin.

"I don't know about this, guys," said Ladi. "I've heard horror stories about these things. I had an uncle who turned into a cockroach in order to play a prank on his wife. Except he couldn't turn back and his family members spent hours trying to squash him to death."

"I could demonstrate, if you'd like?" asked the goblin merchant. "To ensure its safety."

He placed the mask on his face, and Zero watched as he transformed into a statuesque blonde wearing a leopard-print shirt and jeans.

Camih picked up one of the Kobasticker cases and twirled it in her hands.

"We will need four of them," said Camih, and Ladi groaned.

"Sure, madam," said the goblin merchant. His voice had become silky and feminine. "For that many I'll make it a special price. Only three Dark tokens."

"I'll give you two."

The tokens exchanged hands. The goblin peeled off the mask and was once more the hooded, slightly stooping figure who had first appeared.

"Thank you for your business," he said, closing the trolley's panel and bowing low.

The lights in the car began to flicker until the car was plunged into darkness.

When the lights returned, the trolley was gone.

Camih was holding up the four Dark Kobastickers like a hand of cards.

"These Kobastickers are called Degizzenouvox. With these, we have a way to avoid the police once we get on Goldrick. You're welcome," she said, grinning.

The rest of the trip to Goldrick, Zero and the crew spent memorizing the details of their new identities.

"I got Xi Yomi, a middle-aged businesswoman who runs a troll boxing promotion company and apparently has a very messy romantic life. My kind of woman," said Camih.

"I got Ria Romuk," said Efua. "A retired opera singer."

"Lucky you. I got Pepe Pedrinelli. I'm a retired blazeball player with a drinking problem. Who did you get, Zero?" asked Ladi.

"I got a chap called Jamie Smith. He was a whizzer pilot.

His biography just says: 'Doesn't talk much.' Can we swap these?" grumbled Zero.

"No," Camih said firmly. "We'll use these Kobastickers as soon as the announcement is made that we are approaching Goldrick. We don't know how long the operation will last, so we should hold off putting on our disguises as long as we can so we don't go over the time limit. The merchant said the transformations will last two hours, but I think we should plan for one. These Black Rose products can be quite unreliable."

Zero nodded.

"Have you guys ever thought of what you would do with the Mask of the Shaman King once you found it?" Efua asked quietly.

They all looked at her.

"An object that can grant wishes. It could solve all our problems," she continued.

"It grants one wish, so it could only be used by one person," pointed out Ladi.

"We promised we would bring the Mask back to Mrs. Turkoglu so she can carry out the ceremony and free the soul of her daughter," said Zero.

"Not to mention, chances are high that the next time the Mask is used, it will help free Zomon from his prison! I'd rather not see that mass-murdering maniac roaming free," said Ladi.

The train passed through a nebula. For a moment the car was basked in a multicolored glow.

Zero noticed that Efua began to rub her thumb and index

finger together. It seemed to be a habit she had when she was nervous. After a moment she shrugged.

"I understand what you mean, but it's a shame such a powerful object is going to be destroyed, that's all," she said, holding her hands up in surrender.

"Our priority should be to return the artifact to Selima Turkoglu—"

Zero was cut off by the loud screech of a microphone being turned on.

"Ladies and gentlemen: We are now approaching our requested stop of Goldrick. Landing time is approximately fifteen minutes . . ."

Zero stared out his window at a planet with green and purple swirls like a marble.

The train suddenly nosedived, making Zero's stomach lurch. It righted itself quickly before diving once more. The process repeated like a frenzied roller-coaster ride until they broke through the atmosphere of Goldrick.

Just when he thought he could bear it no longer, the space train righted itself for good and floated toward the Goldrick capital.

From up in the sky they glimpsed a giant building in the shape of a golden G towering over the rest of the city.

"That's the Goldrick Bank headquarters," said Ladi.

All around it sprawled a murky gray city.

"The cops are going to expect us to be in a group of four, so we're going to split up. We're each going to get off from a separate car," said Camih.

"We can also use this Kobasticker. It's called Radyondelnix. It establishes a connection between us and lets us all communicate telepathically," added Ladi.

Ladi held out his hand and summoned the Kobasticker. There was a tiny thunderclap as a triangular Kobasticker materialized in Ladi's palm. It had an image of a phone with an antenna that gave off sparks. The Kobasticker shot out blue bolts of light that struck each of them.

Zero looked down at his arm. The Radyondelnix symbol appeared on his skin.

Camih then handed out the Degizzenouvox Kobastickers.

"Remember that summoning a Dark Kobasticker is a little different. Repeat after me: *Yaba-Degizzenouvox*," she said, placing the Kobasticker on her arm.

"*Yaba-Degizzenouvox*," they repeated in unison and placed their Kobastickers on the insides of their forearms.

The masks materialized before them in a cloud of black smoke. Zero plucked his out of the air and placed it over his face.

Zero had not expected it to be so painful. He sat down, fearing he would pass out. He noticed Ladi was on his hands and knees. His nose had grown to the size of a watermelon, and one of his ears was larger than the other.

Camih was bent over the table opposite Zero, and Efua was curled up on the floor.

The pain stopped as suddenly as it had started. When Zero stood up, his first impression was that everything was wrong. Everything seemed farther away than normal. His eyeline was higher, and when he moved his arms, their proportions were unfamiliar. He caught his reflection in the window and almost had a heart attack. A bald man with a bushy beard and small, beady eyes looked back at him.

He looked at the others and couldn't recognize them either.

"Zero, is that you?" asked the tall red-haired woman that was Camih. "Your disguise isn't that bad. You still look cute."

She turned toward Ladi. "Oh my God. Is that you, Ladi? Pardon me for saying so, but you look horrendous."

"No offense taken. Efua?" said Ladi, who was now a man with mottled skin and a bald patch on his head.

"I'm here," said Efua, who was now a short woman. She had twin red spots on her cheeks the size of tennis balls, pigtails, and buckteeth.

"I'm fine. It's just that my teeth hurt," she said, patting her protruding front teeth with the heel of her hand.

The train gave a final wobble as it reached the station.

"All right, I suggest we all have one last good look at each other. Then we split up," said Camih.

"I think I'm set. Although it does hurt when I look at Ladi," said Zero.

"Don't hurt my feelings," said Ladi, smiling and exposing his lack of teeth.

"Let's go," said Efua.

She and Zero headed toward the next car at one end, while Camih and Ladi headed toward the other.

Camih had said to expect a large contingent of police, but this was more than Zero had anticipated.

At every exit, half a dozen officers were stationed and inspecting passengers.

They pulled on beards, searched pockets, and patted down outfits. On the car to Zero's right, a tall troll constable was holding a passenger upside down by the ankles and shaking him.

"Papers," demanded a burly constable.

Zero searched in his pockets and held out the only documents he had. Efua did the same. He passed the man being held upside down and saw the two figures of Ladi and Camih. He locked eyes momentarily with Camih. She gave him a thumbs-up.

With a furrowed brow, the troll was still inspecting the documents they had received as part of the disguises. He had one eye shut, as if looking through the scope of a rifle.

Zero was beginning to feel nervous. Was there a mistake on the documents?

Zero heard a loud shout and turned to see what looked like a snake drop out of the pocket of the man being held upside down. The constable checking Zero's and Efua's papers looked up at the commotion.

"You can go," said the troll, handing back their passes. He told the rest of the line to wait and walked over to assist with the snake.

Zero let out a sigh of relief, and then he and Efua followed the steady stream of passengers all the way out of the train station and onto the street.

They waited in front of the entrance to the station. Across the street was a park with a wide concrete footpath that led to a main square just outside Goldrick Bank.

The streets were filled with hover cars, and above them, hundreds of airships glided past, throwing shadows across the ground like clouds across a grassy plain.

"You guys okay?" asked a voice.

Zero started. He turned to see the transformed figures of Camih and Ladi.

"We don't have that much time left," Efua said. "We had better get this over with."

CHAPTER 17

The streets were lined with never been and the hundreds of as ose boodwa

THE Goldrick Bank headquarters reared up before them. It was an imposing structure, so bright and shiny it seemed to be made of actual gold. The top floors were hidden in the clouds.

The friends made their way to the giant glass doors and into a waiting area where clients were made to pass through twelve metal detectors. In front of the group, a short creature with red skin dressed in a brown kaftan and hat was removing a few grenades from his pockets. He placed them on a tray as the security guards, furry creatures with red skin and overbites, looked on. To their right, a yeti-like creature with blue skin and two giant tusks was reaching into its fur and pulling out a number of weapons it proceeded to add to a pile that already rose many feet into the air. The security guards seemed rather nonchalant about it all. They must have been used to clients appearing with an arsenal on their person.

"Next!" shouted one of the security guards.

Zero jumped and looked at the stern security guards motioning them forward.

Zero walked through the detectors, and alarms went off.

"Just a moment!"

Zero froze as one of the guards walked over to him.

"Sir, I am going to have to ask you to show me your Kobastickers. I'm getting a strange reading from the Koba detector."

Zero took a deep, shuddering breath and shut his eyes.

"I think it might be this," he mumbled, and said the words to materialize Cabbagenix.

The guard squinted at Zero's Kobasticker. "I can't believe it. An actual Cabbagenix! Hey, Bobby, Edwin, come see this!"

Two of his colleagues walked over to see what was going on. They took one look at Zero's Kobasticker, snorted, and motioned to the other guards, who left their posts and rushed over.

Before long, Zero was swarmed by security guards who were sniggering and talking loudly like a group of school-children. They kept asking him if they could take pictures with him. Zero felt so embarrassed he wanted to disappear.

"Please can I go now?" he said.

That seemed to break the spell.

"Y-yes of course," said the first security guard, coughing into his fist in an attempt to regain his composure.

Zero peeled away from the guards, but when he looked back they were still pointing at him and laughing. He caught Ladi grinning and glared at him.

"Don't. Say. A. Word," Zero growled, and Camih winked.

The four friends walked further into the lobby. It was a grandiose room with vaulted ceilings and floors made of dark marble.

It was also teeming with dozens of Space Mafia members in crisp suits, fedora hats, and black sunglasses, puffing on cigars.

In the center of the room, under a lustrous chandelier,

was a giant fountain with a golden statue depicting a strange scene: a man in a double-breasted coat held a wad of cash and was scrutinizing a particular bill.

Zero watched as Ladi pressed two fingers against Radyon-delnix so it began to glow.

Almost instantly, Zero felt a pleasant shudder spread through his body, as if someone were cleaning his ears. When Ladi spoke, his voice seemed to come from inside Zero's head. It echoed inside his skull as if a microphone had been installed inside his brain.

That's a representation of Don Dosco. He was the first head of the Space Mafia and governor of Goldrick Bank. He was famous for his ruthlessness and his aversion to small-denomination bills. This particular statue depicts a scene that happened a few moments before the Paradisio Massacre. Don Dosco was counting his money and found a one-berry note. He proceeded to execute ten of his fifteen lieutenants. We learned about it in Criminal Organization History, explained Ladi.

Gruesome, said Zero.

Can we please focus on the task at hand? asked Camih. She spoke a little too loudly and it made them all wince.

"Ahem," said a voice behind them.

The crew all turned around.

A tall man in black coattails approached them. His name tag read "Jim, Customer Rep."

"Can I help you?" asked Jim the Customer Rep.

"Yes . . . we were looking for an item," said Zero.

"Would you have an account number?"

"Yes. One moment!" said Zero, searching in his pocket. He pulled out the small piece of paper with the code and tried to flatten it on his hip before handing it over.

Jim took it with one gloved hand. With the other, he snapped his fingers and an eyeglass materialized out of thin air. He took hold of it and pressed it against his right eye.

"Yes, that's on the fifth floor. Vault 3. Right this way, if you please," said Jim, slipping his eyeglass into his coat pocket.

The fifth floor of Goldrick Bank was actually underground. They took a golden elevator down. When they exited into the corridor, Zero had the impression that he'd stepped into a war zone.

There was a loud detonation that made the very ground shake and caused a shower of dust to trickle down onto Zero's head.

As he looked down the corridor, Zero saw black smoke pouring out of one of the chambers. The smoke rose to the roof and snaked toward them. A steady stream of Geekaloos ran down the corridor holding buckets of water. A terrible roar shook the air, and Zero thought he saw a giant tail slice out from the burning chamber.

"Was that a dragon?" asked Zero shakily. He and his friends exchanged wide-eyed looks.

Next to the elevators, a potbellied man in a pin-striped suit stood outside a vault. He had a beaked nose and a rose pinned to his pocket and held a cigar. He was haranguing a band of Boolicks.

The little yellow-furred creatures were trembling as they

listened to the man. Their tufted tails wagged anxiously, and a few of them had their furry fingers in their wide beaks.

"Gon?" he yelled. "Gon, where are you? It's your turn!"

A skinny Boolick was pushed unceremoniously to the front of the crowd. He was shaking so much that his knees knocked against each other.

"Ready? One . . . two . . ."

On the count of three, the poor Boolick was shoved inside the vault. The man began shouting instructions.

"Excellent, Gon, remember to dodge the guillotines . . . Excellent! Now don't fall into the crocodile pit . . . Great! Well done! Now you just need to get past the chimera—"

There was a very short "eek" followed by an earsplitting roar, and then a burp.

The Mafia leader dropped his shoulders and shook his head before turning back to the other Boolicks.

"Bong! Bong, you're next!"

The crowd of subordinates gulped as one.

"Welcome to the fifth floor, also called 'the Floor of Trials,'" said Jim formally. "Every vault on this floor requires an additional level of security. Anyone who wishes to retrieve an item from their vault not only must have the exact account number but also must complete a trial in order for the contents to be released."

Zero swallowed. Zero, Camih, Ladi, and Efua followed Jim in silence until they reached a blast door with the number three on it.

"Vault 3, here we are."

Mr. Jim pressed a few buttons on a small keypad and the blast door slid open. The group peered inside. The massive vault had a high ceiling and white marble floors and white walls so bright it hurt to look at them. In the center of the vault was a metal plinth like the tip of a pencil.

"Please let me know if you need anything," Jim said cheerfully. "I will be waiting up in the lobby."

"You're not going to accompany us?" asked Zero.

"Certainly not," said Jim, and with that he turned on his heel and walked away.

For a moment they were all rooted to the spot, until Zero steeled himself and stepped inside the chamber. Camih, Efua, and Ladi followed suit. Zero walked up to the stone plinth. A screen was embedded in the side of the plinth, and it read: *Press Continue.*

"Ready?" Zero asked the others.

They all nodded, bracing themselves.

Zero reached out and pressed the Continue button in the corner of the screen.

The top of the plinth folded away with the sound of churning cogs, revealing a golden scale.

But Zero quickly became distracted by a glass cage that had emerged from a trapdoor a few feet to their left.

The cage was split in two. One half of the chamber was empty, but in the other was a large cat-like creature with blue fur and purple spots. It had long, slanted eyes and serrated teeth.

The creature was lying on its side with one paw scratching its stomach with an air of supreme disinterest.

"Oh, I know what this is," said Ladi. "This is a Spellman trap."

"A what now?" asked Zero.

"A Spellman trap. One person places themselves in the empty compartment of the glass cage. His team members must then balance three magical stones on the scales before the timer runs out. Otherwise, the Neptunian Singing Jabbajaw will be released from its cage. We definitely don't want that," said Ladi.

Zero looked from the Jabbajaw, which was yawning and inspecting its claws, to the golden scales.

He imagined the damage it would be able to do with those teeth.

"The stones are made of a special material that absorbs Koba. The more Koba they absorb, the heavier they become," added Ladi.

Zero read the screen.

"Apparently, the Jabbajaw is named Jeffrey," said Zero. He didn't know why the information made him sweat.

To decide who would enter the glass chamber, they did a few rounds of rock paper scissors. Zero was only half relieved when Ladi came in dead last.

Seeing Ladi approach, Jeffrey the Jabbajaw leapt to its feet and began to pace the glass chamber.

Muttering darkly under his breath, Ladi walked through the door to the cage and closed it behind him.

The screen on the plinth showed a countdown.

2:59 ... 2:58 ...

"All right, we should weigh the stones. They might not weigh the same, and then we'll know which stone we need to infuse with Koba," said Zero.

"Good thinking," said Camih. "Zero, you can weigh them."

He nodded and picked up the stones one by one. The first weighed about as much as an apple. The second felt like a stack of plates, and the third weighed like a coin.

Zero gave Camih and Efua his opinion.

"Okay," Camih said. "Since we can only add weight to the stones, we should put the two heavier stones together and try to make the lighter stone balance their combined weight."

"I agree," said Zero.

"So do I," said Efua.

"All right," said Camih. *"Koba-Blueflash."*

A Kobasticker materialized and Camih placed it on her forearm.

They had a minute and thirty seconds left.

She aimed blue sparks at the smallest stone. It flashed, tendrils of energy crawling across it.

After twenty seconds, Camih stopped and they placed the stones on the scale.

"Still need a bit more," said Zero.

Camih obliged.

There were forty seconds left now, and Ladi was growing impatient. A narrow space had opened up under the divider, and the Jabbajaw was reaching out its paw like someone looking for something under a bed. As it did so, it hummed a popular elven song.

Zero looked at Camih, the glow from Blueflash on her sweat-slicked face. She was growing weaker; what had been a healthy beam narrowed into a tiny, sputtering trickle.

"I think it's fine," said Zero.

Camih stopped and stumbled backward. Efua caught her before she fell.

Zero reached for the last stone.

"No pressure, Zero!" cried Ladi, who was pressing his back against the glass to get as far from the probing paw as possible.

Zero ignored him.

There were only ten seconds left.

He placed the stone on the scale slowly.

The scale tipped down suddenly, and panic was like a red-hot iron rod inside him. But then it rose back up and came to a balance.

There was a loud click somewhere deep within, and the crew watched as the plinth descended through a hole in the ground. Another plinth appeared, holding up a beautiful metal block carved with intricate symbols.

They stood there, mesmerized.

Back in the glass chamber, the Jabbajaw let out a mournful melody.

"Nice going, guys! I always knew you would come through," said Ladi, leaping out of the glass cage.

"This isn't the Mask, is it?" asked Camih.

Efua shook her head.

"No. This the Tear of Kings. It is meant to reveal the resting place of the Mask of the Shaman King."

"So, technically, this is another clue? A map that will lead us to the Mask?" asked Zero, turning the metal in his hand.

He looked up at Camih and his jaw dropped.

"What? What's wrong?" said Camih.

Part of her face looked like it was melting.

"The effects of the Kobasticker must be wearing off. We need to get out of here."

Zero grabbed the Tear of Kings and froze. At the top of the plinth right under where the cup had been, an inscription had been scratched:

ER

"Zero?" asked Efua, touching his shoulder.

"The plinth—" he began.

"We don't have time!" Camih shouted, pushing them both toward the door. "We need to get out of here! Now!"

Out in the corridor, they ignored the medical staff carrying a man on a stretcher who had blue smoke pouring out of his ears.

They kept their heads down as they waited impatiently for an elevator.

Come on, come on, come on, thought Zero.

Finally, the doors dinged opened for a mercifully empty elevator.

They rode the five floors up to ground level in silence. Ladi's violet hair had burst forth from his bald patch, and Efua's own green eyes kept darting to Zero and the Tear of Kings.

They hurried through the lobby as quickly as they could. Jim the Customer Rep was stationed by the entrance, and he glanced at them with a bit too much interest.

Zero dropped his gaze and practically ran through the doors to freedom.

CHAPTER 18

ZERO, Camih, Ladi, and Efua moved quickly through the streets, desperately looking for somewhere safe to inspect the Tear of Kings while their Kobastickers recharged. By now their disguises had evaporated completely, and Zero couldn't help but feel incredibly vulnerable without them.

He was acutely aware of the stares of passersby. Did they recognize him?

They passed men and women in suits, a few joggers, and a raccoon-like beast-man who was busy eating a sandwich on a bench. A cool afternoon breeze sent an old newspaper flying and plucked leaves from the trees.

They were rushing down a sidewalk lined with acacia trees when three black hover cars with tinted windows glided up beside them.

Zero and the others ignored them, picking up their pace. Zero watched as a window was lowered from the middle hover car.

A voice called, "Excuse me, my young friends. Could I please have a word?"

Zero glanced toward the car. A creature with the head of a rhinoceros sat in the passenger seat. He wore black sunglasses, a black suit, and a leery smile.

Zero caught Efua's eye.

"On the count of three, we run," Camih whispered, only loud enough for their crew to hear.

"I wouldn't try anything stupid if I were you, Ms. Sitso." The creature chuckled.

Camih froze and Zero almost bumped into her.

"Do I know you?" Camih asked carefully.

"My name is Sunday, Ms. Sitso. I'm here on the orders of my boss. Someone you know very well. He would really like it if you would join him for lunch."

"And what if we say no?" growled Zero.

Sunday sighed. He raised his hand and a gun glinted in the sunlight, its barrel aimed at Zero. He snapped his fingers with his other hand, and the doors of the cars in front of and behind his flung open. Men in suits poured out, wielding guns that they aimed at the four of them.

"No sudden movements, and nobody go for their Kobastickers unless you want to get hurt," said Sunday.

"And you think you can kidnap us in public? In front of all these witnesses?" asked Camih.

Sunday laughed. He brought two fingers to his lips and whistled loudly.

Zero watched, dumbstruck, as every single bystander on the street walked away from the area.

The raccoon beast-man took a last bite from his sandwich, dumped it in a gray garbage can, and hurriedly crossed the street.

"What was it you were saying about witnesses?" asked Sunday.

Camih raised her hands, surrendering.

Zero, Camih, Ladi, and Efua had their arms tied and were then unceremoniously shoved into the car at the head of the convoy.

The car stopped in front of a squalid redbrick building in a seedy part of town, and the friends were lugged out of the car and bundled inside.

They were taken to a room on the eighth floor that was decked out with antique furniture and paintings. They were all shoved down onto a plush black sofa.

"You summon your Kobastickers, you die," cautioned Sunday, nodding toward the four henchmen standing guard with guns aimed at each of them. "I'll go get the boss."

Sunday left the room, slamming the door behind him. A short while passed before the door opened and a tall man in a blue double-breasted dinner jacket stepped into the room. He had silver hair that fanned out like a feather duster and wore a black monocle. His eyes were sharp and unblinking, like a viper's.

Sunday stood beside the man, flanked by a few of his underlings.

"Rozan," breathed Camih.

"In the flesh."

They watched as Rozan collapsed onto the black sofa opposite them. He crossed his feet and spread his arms across the back of the sofa.

"Camih, how long has it been?"

"Not long enough."

Rozan grinned. He looked like a shark.

"Imagine my surprise when a few of my men saw you

walking outside Goldrick Bank. I just had to extend this invitation to meet."

"If this is how he treats his guests, I wonder how he treats people he has problems with," muttered Zero under his breath.

Rozan clicked his fingers. The door behind him opened and a procession of cooks pushing trolleys filled with food strolled into the room.

Trays were set in front of Zero and the others. The cooks then simultaneously lifted the silver platters to reveal a steaming dish of fried plantains, jollof rice, and gumbo.

"*Bon appétit*," said Rozan as he unfurled a white napkin, placed it on his lap, and began to cut up a steaming turkey leg.

"Who is this guy?" asked Zero.

"That's Rozan Leombre. His father was a former head of the Space Mafia, but he was struck down by a curse that made him fall into a coma. Rozan took over for him."

Zero bristled. The Space Mafia had their hands in everything from trafficking to poaching to illegal space mining. To be sitting across from its head . . .

"He's an incredibly talented Saba," Camih continued bitterly. "He could do a lot of great things, but instead he chooses to use his skills to conduct criminal activities. He was also once friends with Zoe. When I heard Jenkins & Jenkins & Jenkins were sending representatives to all of Zoe's disciples, I was afraid they would go and see him."

"Fortunately, Jenkins & Jenkins & Jenkins don't seem to mind my 'criminal activities.' They gave me Zoe's Nka, same as you."

"What do you want, Rozan?" snarled Camih.

Rozan lowered his knife and fork. The napkin across his lap floated up to his face to dab the corner of his lips.

"I want what it is you took from that vault."

"What makes you think we even took something from the bank?" asked Camih.

"Don't insult me. The Tear of Kings. The little object in the left-hand pocket of your dumb-looking friend on your right."

"I resent that!" cried Zero.

"Camih, I may refuse to read your mind out of principle, but your underlings are another matter. I have to say, if you knew just what type of feelings—"

"DON'T!" shouted Ladi.

Rozan grinned and turned to Zero.

"Or the secrets Camih has been hiding from you, my little friend, which would destroy your faith in her."

Zero looked at Camih.

"Don't listen to him, Zero," she whispered. "He's just trying to get in our heads."

"You see," Rozan continued, "all this talk of the Mask of the Shaman King would have flown over my head, but I made an interesting discovery at the ancient Leombre manor. A book dating back thousands of years that belonged to my ancestor, a certain king"—he clicked his fingers and an old hardcover book flapped onto the table.

"You must be joking. You're a descendant of King Barbus?" Ladi asked.

"The stories always focus on the son," Rozan drawled. "They forget he had a daughter."

Zero felt his heart drop into his stomach.

"How did you even know we would be going to Goldrick?" he asked.

"You underestimate the scope of my power and influence." Something tugged at Zero's mind.

"You were the one who killed the informer!"

"It was a sad mistake," Rozan replied, shaking his head. "We had simply wanted to extract information from him. But one of my underlings let him escape during his . . . interrogation. He decided to kill him to tie up loose ends. But don't worry. I have dealt with the underling in question. He won't be making any more mistakes."

Zero was horrified. "You're a monster."

"Hardly. The real monster is sitting to everyone's left."

He looked past Camih, past Ladi, to where Efua sat at the end of the sofa.

"Thank you, Efua, for your help."

Zero watched, horrified, as Efua slowly got to her feet and walked over to Rozan's side.

"I can't believe it," said Zero. And then he remembered. "Those men at the Flamengo Hotel on Odunsi . . . I kept wondering how they'd heard of the room number clue. It should have been impossible for anyone but Zoe's disciples to know about it . . . unless of course they had been told about it by one of the disciples themselves. They were working for you?"

Efua smiled. "Very perceptive as always. It's a shame you realized it too late."

"I can't believe it," said Ladi.

"You played us for fools," said Camih.

"Do you think Zoe would have betrayed her friends like this?" Zero yelled.

"And how did her morals help her? Dead on a doomed expedition to the Dark Galaxy. If you're hoping to hurt me, don't waste your breath," said Efua.

"Why?" said Zero. "Why did you do this?"

"In order to find my parents, I need resources. And Rozan has promised to give me those resources."

"Lord knows I love some drama," Rozan said loudly, "but I would rather we speed things along, please. Sunday, fetch the Tear of Kings."

Sunday walked over to Zero and reached into his pocket. Zero tried to twist his body away from Sunday, but the brute clubbed him across the head. All the rebelliousness leapt straight out of him.

Sunday pulled out the Tear and returned to Rozan's side. He placed it softly on the table.

Rozan held it up to the light.

"Astonishing!" he said, his eyes bright with greed. "If the legends are true, it will lead me to the Mask of the Shaman King. I will be able to rectify an injustice against me and my family. And help solve whatever problems Efua has. Finding her parents, I suppose," he added breezily.

"I get it now, you want to use the Mask to make a wish to remove the Namakou's curse on your family," said Camih.

Zero looked from Camih to Rozan.

Rozan held her gaze and rolled up one of his sleeves.

Over his arm ran strange black markings that looked like smudged tattoos.

"The curse is affecting you, just like it affected the rest of your family. It's the same curse that was placed on King Brabus as punishment for all the horrible things he did," said Camih.

"Oh, I am certain of it. If I use the Mask of the Shaman King to lift the curse on my family, then both my father and I will be saved. If I somehow release Zomon in the process, imagine how grateful he will be to me for freeing him. And with Zomon on our side, there is nothing that my family will not be able to accomplish. We will reclaim our leadership of the Space Mafia, and the Leombre family will once more reign across the galaxy. That's a win-win situation if ever there was one!"

"Zomon will destroy you!" said Camih.

"Not if I have the Mask of the Shaman King!" gloated Rozan.

"You're insane," said Zero.

Rozan turned to look at Zero and the light went out of his eyes.

When he spoke, his voice was like fiery hot metal.

"Just because I let Camih talk to me like that doesn't mean that you can."

Rozan's eyes filmed over with white and a Kobasticker glowed across the inside of his arm.

Immediately Zero felt an invisible hand fasten itself around his throat and squeeze with all its might. Panic flared in Zero and his consciousness begin to fade.

Then it stopped.

Zero fell forward, clutching his neck.

"I will be taking this with me," said Rozan, holding up the Tear of Kings. All his crew left the room, apart from Efua. "But before I go, here is a little parting gift."

The room was filled with a high-pitched whine. Zero clapped his hands over his ears. The air shook and Zero felt his whole body vibrating as if he were standing on a giant washing machine.

"I call this 'the Dance of Despair.' It overwhelms a victim's brain with its worst memories and forces them to harm themselves and others. It's a little ability I developed thanks to my mega-Kobasticker Andromeda, and it will affect anyone I consider an enemy or a threat."

He rose, dusting off his coat. "I would kill you myself, but there is something about being killed by your own friends that feels more poetic."

Zero felt his hands move without any instructions. He watched, horrified, as they fastened themselves around his own neck and squeezed.

He wasn't the only person having problems controlling his body.

Ladi's hands were reaching for Camih's neck.

"Ladi, if you don't stop right this instant!" screamed Camih, but she couldn't stop her own hands from reaching out to claw at him.

"I . . . can't . . . control my hands!" panted Ladi.

"Goodbye, Camih," purred Rozan.

"You're insane!" screamed Camih.

But Rozan was out the door, followed closely by Efua. She didn't so much as glance in Zero's direction.

And then the voices began.

You'll never be a great Saba.

You're a disgrace to Zoe.

Each word cut at him like a searing knife. His head felt like it was going to explode.

You will amount to nothing.

A familiar scene began to materialize behind his eyelids: a dark silhouette—his mother, setting him on the ground outside Cégolim's walls before turning to leave. Zero screamed and begged her to turn around, but the words sounded as if he were screaming underwater.

The scene changed and now he was sitting on the edge of the Temple of Ifanabe, watching a red whizzer shaped like a phoenix climb slowly into the sky. The whizzer carrying Zoe and Kadj disappeared into the clouds, and he felt sadness flood over him.

The scene changed once more, and this time he was in a desert, standing face-to-face with a girl. She cupped her hand and held it out to him. And when he saw what she held, he felt panic climb up his throat.

Just as Zero was sinking into despair, a voice got through to him:

"Zero! Bud, we could use your help here! You're the only one who can stop this."

"How?" croaked Zero.

"Short . . . circuit!" Ladi's hands fastened around Camih's neck, and she hissed at him.

Zero was nervous. So far, his attempts at mastering Jupiter had been abject failures. But if he did not learn to master it now, they would all die.

"I believe in you, Zero! Listen . . . concentrate. Just don't take too long," added Ladi.

He tried to concentrate, but it was like trying to stand up in a waterfall. The voices in his head were overpowering.

Think, Zero.

He tried to create a small pocket of tranquillity and quiet.

He pictured the Kobasticker and then called out its name: *"Koba-Jupiter!"*

He felt a warmth spread deep inside him like a match being ignited, chasing away the darkness. It was a fragile flame, which flickered dangerously, but it was a flame nonetheless.

It was quickly snuffed out by the noise.

He tried again, but this time the flame was even smaller. He tried once more and nothing happened at all.

Come on! Come on!

His consciousness was fading now. He thought of Camih and Ladi, who were depending on him. He thought, too, of Efua and her betrayal, and of Rozan on his way to steal the Mask of the Shaman King. The utter failure of it all overwhelmed him.

As his consciousness drifted away, he thought: *Somebody, help!*

· · 🗿 · 🐙 · 🦑 · 👹 · 🖐 · 🛸 · 🏚 · 🐜 · 🎎 · ✋ · 🐭 · 🔺 · ·

Zero was standing in front of a large clay building, white like exposed bone. All across its surface were triangular windows. Running up its side were small wooden footholds jutting out like spikes on a cactus.

Above a dark opening, a large neon blue sign read "Thunderstruck Hotel."

The sky all around him was a roiling mass of purple-and-black clouds that flared with silent lightning. Periodically, great bolts would fork down to the ground like incandescent tree roots.

He walked through the opening and into the building.

He was in a large lobby filled with artifacts: wooden masks, spears, metal sculptures, and wicker furniture. Under his feet were black-and-white-checkered tiles, and above him, ceiling fans threw a swirling pattern of shadows around the room. Opposite the entrance, standing on a wooden counter beside a red telephone, a small figure was staring at a television screen in which Zero could see himself in Rozan's room, keeled over. Ladi had his hands fastened around Camih's neck, her eyes bright with terror.

When the figure turned around, Zero gave a shout.

"Wanderblatch!" he cried.

He had on an apron with "Thunderstruck Hotel" written on it and a black leopard-print cap, and was holding a coconut shell with a blue straw sticking out of it. Wanderblatch smiled, flashing a row of sharp teeth.

"How do you do, Zero? I did not expect to see you so soon."

"What happened to you?" asked Zero. The last time Zero

had seen him, he had been a towering presence nearly seven feet tall. Now he was the size of a handbag.

"I exerted myself a bit too much. Not to mention the injuries! Lenoir got me good, so I have been spending my time here, regaining my strength. Don't worry. I'll be back to my full size in no time. Would you care for some coconut juice?" he asked, holding up his coconut shell.

"No thanks. Where am I?"

"You're at the Thunderstruck Hotel."

"I know, but *where* am I?"

Wanderblatch smiled.

"We're inside you. Or rather we're inside the part of you where the Jupiter resides. The Thunderstruck Hotel is the name of the special realm inside Jupiter. Only users of the Kobasticker and its guardians can access it."

"Does it mean I'm . . . dead?" asked Zero.

Wanderblatch seemed to consider this. "No, or you would be a permanent guest here."

Zero wanted to ask if there were other people working in the hotel, but he held his tongue.

Wanderblatch turned and looked back at the screens behind him.

"That is a nasty weapon you are dealing with. A Constellation series Kobasticker, I presume?"

Zero nodded.

"Well, you're going to have to free yourself from its hold then."

"Yes, but how? I can barely move a muscle. It's like my brain has been hacked."

"Right. But with Jupiter, you can control electricity. You can release an electric pulse to override the signals sent by Rozan's Kobasticker. Remember the ten-finger system I used? I'd say a charge with two fingers' worth of power should do it. Three fingers at most."

The telephone beside him began to ring. Wanderblatch picked it up with both hands—the receiver was almost as tall as he was. He listened attentively, nodding a few times. Then he put down the phone.

"Could I interest you in a cup of hot cocoa before you get back?"

Wanderblatch snapped his fingers and a mug slid across the wooden counter toward him.

"It's on the house. A gift from the previous user of Jupiter."

Zero froze. *Detz.* He looked at Wanderblatch and then at the cup of hot cocoa, suddenly not sure whether it was a good idea.

"Go on," urged Wanderblatch.

Zero blew on the cocoa and took a sip. Warmth sluiced through him, and he felt a current of energy shoot up his spine.

Zero looked down at his hands to see sparks traveling across them.

"This should help. You know, he is not very talkative, but I guess this is his way of saying he trusts you with Jupiter, and also his way of apologizing."

"Apologizing? For what?"

"For the hard times you've been having mastering the Jupiter . . . but especially for *this.*"

Wanderblatch pointed at a section of the ceiling right above Zero's head.

Zero looked up just as a bolt of lightning shot down from the ceiling and struck him squarely on the forehead. His mind went blank.

· ⋇ · 🐙 · 👾 · 🧑‍🚀 · 🏆 · 🥘 · 👣 · 🦗 · 🏯 · ✋ · 🐀 · 🔺 ·

When Zero came to, he felt like he had left a bad dream only to return to it at the worst possible moment.

He pressed two fingers against his left hand. A bolt of electricity shot through his whole body and made his head light up like a lighthouse.

He collapsed forward, coughing. He was finally able to move. He saw sparks of electricity dancing over his hands.

Zero looked toward Ladi and Camih. Ladi had both hands around her neck and was apologizing profusely while Camih clawed at his face.

"I don't think we have a choice! Blast him with your Kobasticker!" cried Camih.

"But I'll hurt him!" said Zero.

"Not more than I'll hurt you if I die here!" said Camih.

"Please be gentle," begged Ladi.

Zero aimed two fingers at Ladi and let out a bolt of electricity that struck him in the chest and sent him tumbling over the couch.

Camih gritted her teeth as Zero shot a few bolts of electricity into her body until she sank onto the floor. She was coughing and massaging her neck.

Rozan's spell had been broken.

Zero rushed over to Ladi and helped him to his feet.

"That was a bit too close for comfort," Ladi groaned.

Camih shouted, "He's going to pay for this! How dare he try to get Ladi to kill me!"

CHAPTER 19

THE double blow of Efua's betrayal and Rozan's theft of the Tear of Kings weighed heavy on the trio's minds as they slipped out of the redbrick building. They hid in an abandoned warehouse close to the Saba train station to regroup.

Zero was miserable. He felt responsible for it all. If he hadn't introduced them to Efua, they wouldn't be in this predicament. If he hadn't been so trusting and naïve, perhaps they would still be in possession of the Tear of Kings.

Disappointed, dejected, and with no clear leads, the group agreed with Ladi's suggestion that they head back to Shango Heart headquarters.

They had just enough money for a ticket on the space train to the Dorkenoo asteroid belt.

Using their disguises, Zero, Ladi, and Camih managed to sneak onto the train out of Goldrick. They'd made sure to book one of the sleeping cars so they would not be disturbed.

Once they were alone, they removed their disguises, letting them recharge. Camih suggested that they call Mr. Gauche. Using a Gooober in their car, she dialed the secure line of the Shango Heart Guild. This particular Gooober insisted on plucking a hair from her eyebrows to verify she had permission to contact Mr. Gauche. Soon Mr. Gauche's television screen face appeared in midair above the Gooober. He was neck deep in a bubble bath with a large pink shower cap over the top of his TV head. Soap bubbles floated all around him. As the connection was made, he gave an embarrassed yelp and let a wooden bath brush he was holding plop into the water.

"Camih! Where have you all been! We've been worried. What is the latest?"

Camih filled him in, the heel of her palm pressed over her right eyebrow.

Mr. Gauche nodded solemnly, his screen face showing a fishing boat bobbing up and down in stormy waters.

"I'm sorry to hear about your latest setback. But I think it's a good thing you are heading home. We have been in contact with a few lawyers who have agreed to help prove your innocence. They are pretty optimistic that the charges will be dropped. How is Zero?"

At the sound of his name, Zero waved.

"I'm doing all right, boss," he said.

Mr. Gauche nodded. "You hang in there!" he said, pointing a finger covered in bubbles. "Stay strong, and if there is anything you need from me, just call."

"Yes, Mr. Gauche," said Camih and Ladi in unison before they closed the connection.

Zero and Camih sat on the top bunks opposite each other.

Ladi collapsed onto his bed below Camih in an incredibly realistic imitation of a beached whale and was quickly fast asleep. Every so often he would spasm slightly, sparks playing over his limbs. Zero supposed it was a side effect of Jupiter's lightning.

A television screen embedded above the door to the car

was showing the evening news, and Zero watched as a small dark elf in a bright blue suit read out the headlines.

"There was nothing we could do," murmured Camih, as if reading Zero's mind.

"It still stings. I feel like I should have known about Efua."

Camih shook her head. "She threw us all for a loop. We all agreed to have her on the team. We all share the blame. Besides, I couldn't be mad at you. Without your help, Ladi and I would be goners."

"Thanks, Camih," said Zero. "What was your experience in the Dance of Despair like?"

The car wobbled softly from side to side as the train ambled through space.

For a moment he thought she had not heard him, and he was about to repeat the question when she finally answered.

"It was hard. It made me relive something I feel really guilty about. It involves you."

"Me?"

"Yes."

"Okay," said Zero.

"You're not going to ask me what it is?"

Zero raised a shoulder.

Lenoir had appeared on the television. The elven presenter showed his mug shot and explained that Lenoir had been arrested after he beat up an eighty-year-old woman for asking him a question about his crushing defeat at the hands of some child Sabas on Anansi 12.

"I'm pretty sure you never did anything mean to me," said Zero.

"You don't know what I did."

Zero looked away from the television toward her.

"The reason Zoe never replied to your emails was because of me."

Zero's heart plummeted.

"I was in charge of my sister's Sigmia account," Camih continued. "She had entrusted it to me since she was so busy. You have to understand that I admired my sister. Perhaps not as much as Soraya, but I really loved Zoe and I didn't want to share her. I was jealous. I didn't want her getting so close to anybody else, so I deleted your messages. That's what I was remembering when I was under Rozan's spell. What I did to you was cruel and mean, and I would have been devastated if someone had done that to me . . ."

Zero said nothing.

"I'm sorry, Zero."

He shook his head. "You shouldn't be. I think in your situation I would have done the exact same thing. We both loved Zoe, and we were both very protective of her. I forgive you."

Camih let herself fall back onto her bed in relief.

"Thanks, Zero."

There was a moment of silence and then she sat back up.

"What was your experience of the Dance of Despair?" she asked.

Zero looked up at the ceiling.

"I spent the time thinking of my mother. My mother abandoned me in the City of Children," said Zero quietly. "All the other children lost their parents after the Great Flash.

Their parents never purposefully abandoned them. But my mother chose to leave me in Cégolim. And then I met Zoe, who was like a second mother to me . . ."

Zero curled his fingers into fists. He felt a sharp burn behind his eyes.

"But then she left me too. I know I shouldn't, but sometimes I think about the fact that the two most important people in my life abandoned me. It's like everyone I care about leaves me eventually."

The words echoed around the small train car.

"I'm so sorry, Zero," said Camih.

"Don't be. I think a part of me thought that if I was successful enough, then my mother might hear about me. She might remember me and want to find me once more. I used to think perhaps it was my fault. But now not so much."

Zero lay down and turned on his side so his head was resting on his forearm. Down below them, Ladi stirred.

Zero remembered something else from Rozan's spell and smiled.

"What?" asked Camih.

"Rozan's spell also showed me an embarrassing memory from my childhood I've been trying to forget. It's actually funny now that I think about it."

Camih smiled.

"Tell me."

"No way! It's way too embarrassing."

"You really shouldn't have said that. Now I *have* to know. Is it something silly you did?"

"Maybe."

"Is it . . . about a girl?"

"Let it go, Camih," Zero laughed. "I'd rather be eaten by a space dragon than tell you."

On the television, a special report was airing about an art collector and businessman called Arsene Ramondo who was organizing a big party that evening at his private palace. He claimed he would be making an announcement with galactic implications.

"Is it something you did to someone?"

"No!"

"All right then, how about I tell you something embarrassing about me in exchange?"

"No deal."

But then Zero thought of something. He looked at her again.

He wished he hadn't. Her gaze had the intensity of a blast furnace.

"What was Detz like?"

Camih was quiet for a bit. "If I tell you about Detz, you'll tell me your embarrassing story?"

Zero thought about it.

"To be honest, I still don't think I would. It's too embarrassing."

"But you don't know what I'm going to tell you. It could be worth your while," she said with a mischievous sparkle in her eyes.

Zero sat up. His heart was beating as if he'd narrowly escaped an encounter with a four-eyed Uranian leopard.

His eyes were glued to the television, wide in shock.

"What is it?" Camih asked, following his gaze.

"Look at the trophy cabinet behind that man. Tell me what you see in the top right corner," said Zero.

Camih squinted.

"It does look identical to the Tear of Kings, but it must be a replica."

"Ever since we beat the trial at Goldrick Bank, something has been bothering me."

"Go on."

"The Tear of Kings is made of metal, right?"

"Of course. You held it, didn't you?"

"But the Tear of Kings we removed from the vault did not conduct electricity!"

"I'm not sure I follow you," said Camih carefully.

"Whenever I touch anything metallic, I know it immediately. I can feel a slight pulse of electricity run through it from the Jupiter. And when I handled the Tear of Kings, I never felt a pulse. It was not metallic."

"Wait, you think it's a fake?"

"Perhaps. And there's something else. When I picked up the Tear of Kings in the vault, there was an inscription scratched on the top of the plinth. The initials ER."

"ER?" Camih asked, her brow furrowing.

Zero nodded. "Have you ever heard of Erena Rosamond?"

"The famous art thief?" Realization was dawning on Camih's face.

"Why didn't you tell me this sooner?" she asked excitedly.

"Didn't really get the chance!"

"And you think the real Tear might have somehow made its way into Arsene Ramondo's collection?"

"I think that Erena Rosamond and this Arsene Ramondo might be connected."

"How so?"

"Their names."

Zero pushed the covers off himself and jumped down from his bed. He ran to one of the bedside tables, took a pen, and scribbled furiously on a sheet of paper. He showed it to Camih.

He had written "Arsene Ramondo" and "Erena Rosamond."

"Erena Rosamond is an anagram of Arsene Ramondo."

CHAPTER 20

ZERO'S discovery reenergized Camih. She jumped down from her bunk and began to pace up and down the car furiously.

"That is incredible. If this is all true, Rozan and Efua would have taken the fake Tear of Kings. The race to find the Mask is still wide open, and Arsene's announcement is tonight." Camih beamed at Zero. "This is one party I can't wait to crash!"

They woke Ladi up and told him about their theory.

"Please don't tell me we are going to have to use our disguises again," groaned Ladi.

"Not unless you would rather be arrested! I do want to remind you that there is still a warrant out for our arrest," said Camih.

"I thought that Mr. Gauche was having that overturned."

"He is, but I'm sure Inspector Priya won't hesitate to put us in jail until then. I'll go request our new stop."

When she got back, they began to plan.

"The train will drop us at Herbert's Rock station, which is less than a mile from Arsene Ramondo's palace." She pointed on the Gooober's map. "We should arrive at the station in two hours. From there we'll just take a space taxi using the Spacecab application," she said, as if it were the most natural thing.

Zero, Ladi, and Camih took the time to rest and recharge their disguises. On schedule, the train began to draw to a stop. Out the window of their car, Zero saw a solitary train stop consisting of a platform the length of a single space shuttle, a ticketing office, and a lone traffic light. There was a wrought-iron sign above it that announced "Herbert's Roc." Zero wondered what had happened to the k.

Zero, Camih, and Ladi donned their disguises and stepped onto the platform, watching the train pull away from the station.

"How far is the taxi?" asked Ladi

Camih checked the Gooober she'd snuck out of the train.

"Five minutes away."

"Perfect," said Zero, who was staring at the creature manning the ticket booth. It had purple skin and a face like a scaly octopus. It was presently fast asleep, its head lolling against the back of his seat. A giant snot bubble was forming in its left nostril. Zero supposed he must not get many customers in this corner of the galaxy.

Soon enough, a yellow taxi drew up to the station. To say it looked like a mechanical carcass was an insult to perfectly respectable mechanical carcasses around the galaxy. The taxi looked like an exploding junkyard on wheels. Its body was made up of hundreds of metal sheets stuck together and painted over. It was four-wheeled with short wings and jet propulsors that coughed black exhaust as the taxi came to a stop. The driver, a kind-faced blond man wearing a red feather hat, beamed at them.

Zero and Ladi looked at Camih.

"It was the only one I could find!" she said defensively.

The taxi was already brimming with passengers. A

number of grumpy-looking beast-men were squeezed in the backseat. Somehow the driver managed to find space for Zero, Camih, and Ladi, though it was at the expense of their ability to breathe. Zero was so squashed between a lion-man and a rhinoceros-man that he felt their huge bodies pressing against his ribs every time either of them breathed. Zero could almost hear his organs crying out for help.

The trio sat in silence as the taxi driver recounted the story of how his fourth wife left him after thirty-three years together for an elven gym instructor living on the planet Luxor. The passengers all nodded politely. Only Ladi seemed to be truly engrossed in the man's story and kept asking him questions.

"We're almost at Arsene Ramondo's palace," said the driver after a while.

Out the window, Zero could see a giant glittering building made of glass. A big electric sign advertised "Ramondo's Big Reveal," and giant spotlights lit up the palace. A flat strip leading to the imposing glass entrance was decorated with a long red carpet, which was lined by masses of photographers cordoned off by velvet ropes.

As the taxi approached, Zero saw two burly security trolls checking the guests' invitation cards and a long line of luxury space cars that stretched out in front of the landing strip as guests were dropped off.

Camih paid the fare after the taxi dropped them off at the red carpet. Up ahead, a few guests were being turned away.

"We're from *Daily Stardust* magazine," one of the women protested. "We have our press badges. Look!"

"I know, but I can't let you in. Mr. Ramondo did not appreciate your piece putting him thirteenth on the Most Influential Art Collectors in the Galaxy list, behind Bourbon Stellois! Next!"

As they moved closer, Zero saw a well-dressed couple oozing luxury and contempt step forward.

"Sorry, you can't come in."

"B-but we're childhood friends! Peter Bopplepop!"

"Not anymore, I'm afraid. Mr. Ramondo gave specific instructions not to let you through. You failed to buy a copy of his wife's latest album."

"This is an outrage!"

The old man grabbed his wife and they walked away.

Zero was worried. What if they got turned away? He didn't like their chances of forcing their way into this heavily fortified venue.

"I think today might be our lucky day," said Camih, smiling.

"How so?" asked Zero.

"I know the bouncer. Follow me."

Zero and Ladi followed closely behind Camih. She walked confidently up to the troll with the invitation list.

"Names, please?" he asked without lifting his head.

"It's been a long time, Flatfoot," said Camih.

"I beg your pardon?" asked the troll, finally looking up from the guest list.

"You don't remember me?"

Camih motioned to him to get closer.

The troll leaned closer and Camih ran her palm over her

face so that her real face appeared for an instance before her disguise reasserted itself like water filling a hole.

The troll did a double take.

"No!" he said, raising a hand to his heart.

Camih grinned wickedly and then said, "Funny seeing you here. I wonder if Mr. Ramondo knows that you like to steal precious belongings from your employers."

"Please, don't say anything."

The other troll noticed Flatfoot's distress and came closer.

"Is everything okay?" he asked Flatfoot. "What's the holdup? Who are they?"

"N-no one. I mean, they're on the guest list," he added when Camih lifted an eyebrow.

He stepped aside and let Camih, Zero, and Ladi walk through.

"What was that all about?" asked Zero once they had entered Ramondo's palace.

"A lucky coincidence. I met the troll while on a mission for the Royal Family of Dark Elves on Nebula 12. I caught Flatfoot stealing their jewelry and promised not to tell as long as he left of his own accord. Now sharpen up, boys. We're in. We need to find the Tear of Kings before the disguises are up."

They found themselves in a giant atrium, which was the glittering part of the palace they could see from the taxi. A podium had been fitted on a stage in the center of the room, with pictures of Arsene Ramondo plastered across the front. A few technicians were sorting out the sound equipment as the guests were served palm wine and finger foods by smartly dressed servants. People mingled happily and chatted noisily around the base of the stage.

"Before we do anything, I need to go to the bathroom," said Ladi, and disappeared through the crowd in search of a toilet.

Zero was beginning to stress. He sincerely hoped that his hunch proved correct. Otherwise, Rozan and Efua would have gotten all the closer to finding the Mask of the Shaman King, while Zero and the others would have wasted their time.

Camih, meanwhile, was having a bit of a situation with a guest who was apparently the ex-boyfriend of the person she had disguised herself as. A small crowd was gathered as the man rattled off a list of grievances he believed Camih had committed.

"She would make me baked beans. Every. Single. Day. For twelve years!" he said, gesturing to the crowd, which responded with a mixture of sympathetic sounds and outraged gasps.

When Ladi returned, Camih seized her exit.

"What were you doing? You could have hurried up!" she complained.

"Were you having a bit of relationship drama?" crooned Ladi. "You should thank me. I think I found where the Tear of Kings might be."

There was a screech as a microphone was turned on, and the lights dimmed. The chatter of the crowd died down.

"This way!" whispered Ladi.

They sneaked up a flight of marble stairs onto a landing that led to a long corridor. They passed the bathrooms and crept to the end of the corridor, carefully spying around the corner.

Down the corridor, two more burly trolls were standing guard next to a red door. They were having an animated discussion about whose biceps were bigger.

"I'll bet that's where Ramondo is keeping the Tear of Kings," said Ladi. "I'm calling dibs on taking out the trolls." He rolled up the sleeve on his right hand and a Kobasticker began to glow on his arm.

"Wait. I'll do it," said Zero.

They both turned and looked at him.

"All right, Zero does it and that's final," said Camih.

Zero nodded.

"Let's see how you manage it. Remember what the Sabas' strategy is?" she said.

Zero remembered. The elegance of a technical Saba was to use the simplest combination of Kobastickers possible.

He took a deep breath and said the words to materialize the Kobasticker he'd bought on Odunsi.

"Wait, is that *Puddlenix*? It is, isn't it! I'm liking this already!" said Ladi, rubbing his hands together.

Zero ignored him and pressed the Kobasticker to his skin.

A flow of water began to trickle down onto the floor from his wrist.

As it pooled, Zero found that he was able to move the water around with his mind. He caused a little thread to loop around the corner toward the trolls.

He knew the water had reached the trolls when they stopped arguing.

"Who left a tap on?" asked one of the trolls.

That was Zero's cue.

He activated Jupiter and crouched down to the ground. He pressed three fingers into the puddle of water.

And sent a tidal wave of electricity coursing through the trolls' bodies.

CHAPTER 21

THE trolls were still twitching when Zero, Camih, and Ladi reached them. Slowly they opened the door and then carefully stepped over the unconscious trolls, who had wreaths of smoke curling out of their ears.

"*Koba-Lightorbnix*," said Camih.

A Kobasticker appeared in her palm. She took it and brushed it along her forearm like a match. There was a sound like the kindling of tinder and Zero watched, entranced, as the Kobasticker burst into flames and collapsed into a bright ball of light that rose to the ceiling.

They were in a large bedroom. A four-poster bed took up the right-hand side, a lounge area sat to the left, and a bay window faced them, opposite the door.

Zero recognized the room immediately. Or rather, he recognized the wooden shelves behind the seating area. That had been where he'd seen the Tear of Kings on TV.

But the Tear wasn't there now. The shelf where he had seen it was empty.

"Where do you think he put it?" mused Ladi.

Zero shrugged.

Camih used the orb of light to illuminate a steel safe next to the bed.

Camih looked at Ladi. "Gotta start somewhere."

He nodded.

"*Koba-Zoutivole*," said Ladi, and materialized a square-shaped Kobasticker that looked like a doctor's bag with an eye mask across it. Ladi pressed it against the inside of his forearm and a purple pouch shot out of his palm. He caught it before it struck the ground.

"My professional tools. Learned all this from the Blueknife Guild while I was still studying. They're all cat burglars and gentlemen thieves," Ladi explained.

Zero watched Ladi pull out a tub of talcum powder. He shook some into a pile in his right hand and knelt down. He blew at his palm, as if blowing a kiss.

Zero watched the plume of talcum powder swirl against the safe. As it settled, he gasped.

The talcum powder had outlined the fingerprints on the keypad where someone had touched four keys. The passcode.

Camih's eyes were glowing with glee, and she was drumming her fingers together excitedly.

Ladi exhaled shakily. The one thing the talcum powder did not tell him was in what order the buttons had been pressed.

He tried one possible passcode, but it failed.

Ladi went through several rounds, each failure sending Zero's heart beating ever faster.

Finally, there was a loud buzz and a delicious click as the safe swung open.

Zero, Camih, and Ladi exchanged looks. Zero reached over and opened the door wide. He glimpsed towering stacks of bills, an ostentatiously large diamond, and, in the corner, the Tear of Kings.

"Zero, you were right again!"

Zero picked up the Tear. It was cool to the touch, and he felt the familiar pulse that told him it was metallic.

There was no mistake this time. They had the right one.

"Are you guys seeing this?" asked Ladi.

Zero looked toward where he was pointing. The soft light from Camih's orb shone on the Tear of Kings, causing an image to be projected on the floor beneath it.

"The light filtering through the Tear's etchings is projecting something onto the floor. It looks like . . . a map. Bring the light closer," said Zero.

The shapes illuminated on the floor turned crystal clear.

"That's a map, all right," said Camih. "I think we just found the location of the Mask of the Shaman King, guys," said Camih.

"What's written in the bottom right corner of the map?" Ladi asked.

Zero squinted.

"It looks like the word 'elipse.'"

"'Eclipse,' more like," said Camih.

"Sounds right. Do you have any idea what this place is?" said Zero, nodding toward the map.

"I think I recognize it. It looks like a location around Atchani. In fact, I'm pretty sure it is Atchani—"

Camih broke off, and Zero froze.

They heard voices outside.

"Boss . . . the guards at the door are passed out," said a low, oily voice.

"Probably asleep on the job. Give them the medicine, boys," said a second voice. It sounded bossy and oddly familiar . . .

There came two loud thuds.

"That should do it," said the familiar voice.

"Under the bed!" whispered Ladi.

Camih extinguished her light. Instinctively, Zero pushed the safe shut and tucked the Tear into his jacket. There was a mad scramble as Zero, Camih, and Ladi dove under the bed just as the door to the room swung open. Yellow light stretched out across the floor in front of the bed.

Three pairs of shoes stepped into their line of sight.

"All right, boys, we stick to the plan. We steal the diamond Mama Dabi wanted and anything of value, and then we skedaddle," said the familiar voice.

Just our luck. Thieves! thought Zero.

"You might want to have a look at this, K. The safe's already unlocked," said a third voice.

"What do you mean?" demanded the voice called K.

"Someone lifted prints, boss. Look!" said the third voice.

Before Zero could stop her, Camih slipped out from under the bed and confronted the thieves.

"Not another move," she growled. "I've got a very powerful Kobasticker aimed at you, and if you so much as sneeze, I'm blasting you into next year."

Zero heard the thieves drop their weapons.

Zero and Ladi scrambled out from under the bed to join Camih.

"Turn around now," she ordered. "Slowly. Take off your masks."

The thieves obeyed.

"Khabib!" cried Ladi.

Khabib sucked his teeth.

"I thought you boys were going straight," Camih yelled. "Weren't you trying to be a real guild?"

Khabib shrugged. "Yeah, but old habits die hard. And besides, who says no to an easy buck?"

Zero opened his mouth to retort, but just then they heard the sound of footsteps approaching down the corridor.

"Someone knocked out the trolls!" said a voice.

Zero turned and looked at Camih.

"Hide!" she whispered.

Every soul in the room ducked for cover. There was a great deal of shoving, arguing, and gratuitous comments about weight gain as the two groups tried to squeeze under the bed.

The door opened and they all fell silent.

"Troll security guards are not what they used to be . . ."

At the sound of the voice, Zero froze. He knew that voice. It made Zero feel like a scorpion was climbing up the back of his neck.

"Sunday," breathed Zero.

"How could they *know*?" Camih answered in a whisper.

"Make sure they don't wake up for a while, if you know what I mean," said Sunday. "That'll teach them to fall asleep on the job."

There was a shuffle of feet followed by two resounding *whams*.

Poor trolls, thought Zero.

From under the bed, they saw shoes sweep toward the security vault.

"If they think they can just walk in here and take my loot—" began Khabib.

"*Our* loot," corrected Zero under his breath.

"Boss, I think someone's already been here," said a voice.

"Don't tell me—" began Sunday.

Before Sunday could get in another word, there was a swell of movement from under the bed as the two groups rolled out and got to their feet.

"Don't move a muscle!" shouted Camih, Zero, and Khabib all at once.

Khabib had a Kobasticker glowing on his arm and his palm trained on Sunday.

Sunday and his underlings raised their hands.

The overhead light turned on.

Arsene Ramondo stood in the doorway, flanked by Efua and Rozan.

At the sight of Efua, Zero felt a cold panic spread through his core. She barely glanced in his direction.

"What's all this racket?" Arsene demanded. "You guys just spoiled my big reveal! The moment I have been working toward all these years! I was going to finally reveal to the world that I am Erena Rosamond, cementing my place as the most famous thief in the galaxy! You've ruined it!"

He looked from the open safe back to them. "Hey, what are you doing with my stuff?"

Rozan stepped around him, grinning at Camih.

"I see you managed to survive our previous encounter."

"I don't know what is stopping me from strangling you right now," said Camih.

"We should hurry up and collect the Tear of Kings, Rozan," said Efua.

Rozan nodded. He turned to Mr. Ramondo.

"Mr. Ramondo, please leave us while we sort out a few things."

"Leave? B-but it's *my* house! They are stealing *my* property!" Arsene objected.

Rozan nodded to a few of his underlings, who promptly escorted Mr. Ramondo out of the room. His complaints faded down the corridor.

"I don't know what is going on right now, but nobody is leaving this place with anything unless it's us with the contents of that safe, so everybody needs to calm down," rambled Khabib.

"How did you know we would be here?" asked Zero.

"It was all thanks to Efua," Rozan said. "Apparently, you three judged it fit to create a psychic link with her during one of your missions."

He flicked his index finger and the Tear of Kings floated out of Zero's jacket and into Efua's hands.

"You have got to be joking!" groaned Ladi.

"She managed to corrupt it and has been able to listen to your conversations ever since."

As if to demonstrate, Efua held up her hand. A Kobasticker appeared there, and the moment she pressed it, an identical symbol appeared on the wrists of Zero, Camih, and Ladi. It blinked once and then vanished.

"You've been outsmarted again, Camih. But you must be used to that by now. Nevertheless, I owe you all a debt of gratitude. Without you, we might never have known about the fake Tear of Kings. And because of that, I won't kill you. Tie 'em up, boys."

Rozan's men grabbed the young Sabas and tied them to the bedposts with rope.

Zero jerked against his bindings, but Rozan merely laughed.

"I think our work here is done," he sneered.

He and Efua left the room, with their underlings and Sunday in tow.

"How do we get out of these?" Khabib groaned, pulling against his bindings.

"Zero! We need you right now, bud!" said Ladi. "Fry these ropes!"

Zero shut his eyes. *Koba-Jupiter.*

He rolled two fingers and pressed them against his palm.

The electric shock made his teeth snap together and the top of his scalp tingle, but it burned through the ropes around his wrists. He was free.

He quickly moved to Camih, then Ladi, burning through their bindings.

By the time he reached Khabib, through the bay window, he could see a sleek black whizzer blast off in the distance.

Rozan. They're getting away!

Zero pressed two fingers against Khabib's bindings, making quick work of them. Khabib gave a sigh of relief and fell back on his back.

"What was that? W-what did you do?"

"It's complicated."

"That was a lightning-based ability. You wouldn't happen to be the owner of the Jupiter, would you?"

Zero nodded without thinking. Behind him, Camih coughed loudly.

"Where is Rozan?" she asked.

"Gone. They took their whizzer," said Zero.

"They really got us," said Camih. She smacked the bedpost with her palm.

Zero heard the click of a gun being cocked.

He turned around to find Khabib with a gun pointed at them.

"What are you doing, Khabib?" asked Camih slowly.

"Making the most of a bad situation."

"This is not the moment to be settling old grudges!"

"That boy is the new owner of the Jupiter!"

Zero looked from Camih to Khabib. He saw the look of horror on Camih's face as she realized Khabib's plans.

"You can't be serious."

"Oh, but I am. I know all about the legend of Jupiter and its thirteenth user. You guys are coming with us. I will be offering the Jupiter as a present to Mama Dabi," he said, grinning.

The room was suddenly flooded with light. A whizzer appeared on the balcony outside, its spotlight trained on the room.

"You guys are really making a big mistake," warned Camih.

"Just the sort of thing you'd say in your position. Move it!" ordered Khabib.

Zero felt the barrel of a gun ram into his ribs as the trio were herded out the balcony doors.

Khabib chuckled to himself. "Oh, Mama Dabi is going to love seeing you again, Camih."

CHAPTER 22

ZERO felt terrible. They had finally managed to determine the location of the Mask of the Shaman King *and* had gotten the upper hand over Rozan and Efua, only to have everything yanked away.

Rozan and his crew were on their way to finding the Mask, while Zero and his crew were being carted off to Mama Dabi's hideout.

Zero felt a knot of frustration in his gut as they boarded Khabib's whizzer named the *S.W. Wolfman*. It looked like a floating wolf's head that wore angular sunglasses and had its tongue lolling out.

The rest of his crew seemed to feel the same.

Camih hid her face in her hands, while Ladi was thumping his head softly against the back of the seat in front of him.

Khabib and his underlings, meanwhile, were behaving like they'd won the intergalactic jackpot for the third time in a row.

They were shouting over hip-hop music so loud it made the seats shudder. Their loud guffaws and juvenile jokes rang irritably in Zero's ears.

Camih's attempts to reason with Khabib fizzled out like ice crystals in a blast furnace.

"We told you our mission could affect the fate of the galaxy. If we don't stop this item from falling into the wrong hands, it could free Zomon, and yet you guys are only thinking about bringing the Jupiter to Mama Dabi."

Khabib shrugged.

"I can't believe you're actually that stupid, Khabib," Camih snapped.

"You're hurting my feelings, Camih, you really are. But we've reached the hideout; so it's too late in any case," said Khabib.

From the whizzer, Zero glimpsed a giant structure protruding from an asteroid. It was the face of a woman wearing large spectacles and a very large purple-and-gold-patterned head tie. The figure looked like a drowning woman crying for help, the lower half of her mouth submerged in the rock.

They entered the headquarters through the statue's mouth. A series of overhead lights lit up a tunnel that led deeper into the lair.

Khabib steered the whizzer past stalactites slick with moisture, on which slept clusters of bats. Finally, they came to a stop on an elevated platform, on which was painted the Scorpiodukes' insignia. The landing pad was fenced in by metal handrails.

When Khabib escorted them out of the whizzer with their hands bound behind their backs, they were greeted by a throng of young Dabi family members, all in brown leather clothes.

Everywhere Zero looked, he saw eager young faces staring back at him. They crowded around the incoming crew, and a few reached out to touch them.

Khabib led them down another tunnel, where even more members of the Dabi family were waiting.

Camih shifted closer to Zero and whispered to him, "They are going to try to intimidate us, but don't be taken in by anything they do."

Zero was wondering what these children could possibly do to intimidate him when the ceiling lights flickered and blinked out.

When they came back on, Zero got a shock.

A collection of human-sized beasts were now standing where the roguish-looking children had been. Humanoid foxes, wolves, and bears with shiny black beads for eyes leered at him. Their hideous forms threw threatening shadows against the concrete walls of the tunnel.

All together, they let out a terrible yowl that shook the very air and made a spear of fear shoot through Zero's insides.

In his shock, Zero bumped into Khabib. It felt like he'd walked into a boulder.

"Ow!" complained Zero, rubbing his shoulder.

He looked up, and where Khabib had been, a giant wolf creature with bulging muscles and white fur leered down at him.

Zero let out a yelp, but Camih placed a calming hand on Zero's shoulder.

"Are you done? Your shape-shifting Kobastickers do not impress us."

"You're no fun, Camih," grumbled the wolf that was Khabib before shifting back to his human form.

Khabib took them down a long corridor, which ended in a small room where a few railcars waited for them, the Scorpiodukes' logo painted on their sides in lime green.

"Get in," said Khabib unceremoniously, and they all climbed in, two per car.

Zero had barely sat down when the cars shot forward and they went whizzing down the tracks, the wind whistling in Zero's ear and making his cheeks ripple and his eyes water. Just as Zero felt like he was about to be sick, the railcars began to slow down. They went past a few doorways with bright wooden signs that read "Thinking Room" or "Nap Room." They eventually passed an "I'd Talk If I Were You" room, which had a drawing of a man with a whip standing next to a man tied to a stake. They finally came to a stop at a doorway that had no sign above it, but Zero could see a row of jail cells through the opening. He knew exactly where they were.

"Everybody off," said Khabib.

He shoved Camih, Ladi, and Zero into a small cell opposite an old man who appeared to have lost his marbles. He was running around his cell with his arms out like a child imitating a plane. Khabib put Zero and Camih together, and Ladi was placed in a cell with a black-haired man with tattered clothes and oily eyes. His face was covered in black soot, as if he'd just emerged from a warehouse full of exploding dynamite.

"Why do I have to stay with this guy?" mumbled Ladi.

"Shut up. And if I were you, I wouldn't buy anything he tries to sell you. He tried to sell us a Kobasticker he claimed could deflect laser beams. We're still trying to put out the fire in the chamber where he did his demonstration."

"Wait! You're the guy from Rokimi & Sons we saw on Odunsi!" said Ladi.

The man smiled sheepishly. His pencil mustache had apparently been singed off.

"You are to wait here until Mama Dabi is ready to receive you," Khabib told the trio.

"We saved your life, Khabib. Don't forget that," said Camih.

"The way I see it, we saved your life too. How exactly did you expect to leave Arsene's palace?"

"No matter what you say, you know it's true. You owe us."

"Suit yourself. If I were you, I would rest up. And don't try anything stupid."

With that, Khabib and his crew turned on their heels and left. They heard the sound of the steel railcars rattling down the train tracks.

"Rozan's probably figured out where the Mask is, and we're stuck here unable to stop him," muttered Zero miserably.

Camih walked over and sat down next to him, wrapping her arms around her knees.

They sat in silence, and Zero stared at a corner of the ceiling.

"A beetle," said Zero after a while.

Camih looked at him, confused.

"The embarrassing moment. It had to do with a beetle. There was this girl I had a crush on back in Cégolim called Zainab. All the boys were in love with her. One day I asked her out, and she said she would give me her answer the following day. So the next day we met just outside the city."

As he spoke, Zero could almost see the clear blue skies dappled with fleecy clouds and feel the dry desert wind blowing over his skin.

"She asked me if I would always love her, and I said I would. She asked me if I would do anything for her. I said I would. She said she wanted me to prove it, to make a show of loyalty to prove that I would never be with anybody but her. So I looked around for something, like a stone or a stick so she could knight me like in the movies. But all we found was a beetle. She held it out to me and told me to eat the beetle if I loved her. So I did. Unfortunately, some boys from Jude's gang were spying on us. They teased me mercilessly after that."

Camih burst out laughing. Despite his embarrassment, Zero joined in too.

For a moment they forgot that they were trapped in a jail cell.

Camih fell silent, her gaze running along the floor and settling on a corner of the room.

"Detz was a young Saba from a famous guild that is a rival to Shango Heart," she said softly after a while. "He was an incredibly talented Saba destined to become one of the supernovas. He was my first great love. He died protecting his guild from an ambush by a sect of anti-Sabas."

"I'm so sorry," said Zero. His heart ached for Camih.

She shook her head. "It was a while ago. I want you to believe what I'm about to say, otherwise I'll be hurt."

"I trust you," said Zero.

"I think of Detz often, but I never confuse the two of you. He was his own person, and so are you, Zero. You have to believe me when I say that." She took a deep breath. "But I also want to make sure that you're not comparing me to Zoe."

Zero was stumped.

"That is important to me."

Zero nodded, feeling a patch of affection spread through his core. "I promise I won't compare you," he swore.

"Close your eyes," said Camih.

She leaned in close.

Zero closed his eyes. He could smell her scent. He felt her arms wrap around his neck. Then he felt her lips press against the corner of his mouth.

His eyes snapped open.

He was rooted to the spot as if Jupiter had sent a current coursing through him.

She pulled away, and he watched as she opened her eyes and watched him like an artist inspecting her finished work.

"When this is all over, we'll have our first kiss. Don't mess it up. I may or may not be looking forward to it," she said, her eyes sparkling with mischief.

CHAPTER 23

THEY heard the sound of metal scraping against metal as the railcars came to a stop at the entrance to the jail cells. A few minutes later, a tall, skinny boy with green hair appeared.

"Mama Dabi will see you," the boy said curtly.

He guided them into the railcars, which rushed farther into the mine until they came to a stop at a doorway simply labeled "Mom."

The skinny boy led them off the railcars and into a large chamber where a woman was waiting for them.

Mama Dabi was sitting on a peacock chair at the head of a long, rough-hewn table. She must have been a tall woman—her torso towered over the table. She wore a blue kaftan with a matching head tie, and in her lap sat a large black cat with a streak down its back like a skunk. Mama Dabi's calm, kind eyes peered at them from behind a pair of spectacles. Their warmth belied the fact that she was one of the most fearsome space bandits in the whole galaxy.

The cat looked lazily at the company and yawned.

It was Zero's first time meeting a guildmaster other than Mr. Gauche. He wondered if any other guildmasters were as imposing as Mama Dabi.

Khabib was standing beside her, tugging at her sleeve.

"Mom, please let me skewer Camih," he groveled. "Please,

Mom? You promised! Just a few holes? I'll use the torture kit you gave me for Christmas. Pretty please?"

"That is enough, Khabib," scolded Mama Dabi.

Khabib let go of her sleeve and turned to face Zero, Camih, and Ladi. He looked like a schoolboy just told off by a teacher.

"Camih," said Mama Dabi. "So you have returned."

"Yes, Mama Dabi."

"There has not been a day when I haven't thought about how you abandoned us, or what we would do to you if we ever found you. I should hang you for what you did!"

This seemed to brighten up Khabib. He began to gesture to a red-haired boy behind Zero who scuttled out of the room. A few seconds later, a wooden contraption with a noose hanging from a beam was rolled in. Zero gulped.

Camih ignored them.

"I needed to move out to discover myself. I needed to grow," said Camih.

"And you couldn't do that here? You needed to join the guild of that hopeless dreamer Mr. Gauche? Don't make me laugh!" she sneered, her words venomous. "I should have you gunned down right this minute!"

Khabib rubbed his hands together eagerly, and motioned to the red-haired underling who'd brought the wooden hangman to take it away. He returned a few moments later with a steel briefcase and opened it to reveal a glistening selection of guns. Khabib looked pleadingly at Mama Dabi.

"But you won't, because you know I can be useful to you, Mama Dabi," Camih replied firmly. "And I have a deal for you."

Mama Dabi scoffed. "You insult me."

"I saved Khabib's life!" Camih protested. "He was going to get himself killed by members of the Space Mafia and we saved him."

"Well then, you have only yourself to blame. You were always too forgiving, Camih. Too naïve. Nonetheless, I am ready to overlook that because my son has told me something interesting about you and your friends."

Zero shifted his weight from one leg to the other.

"The Jupiter. It seems that the legendary Kobasticker has found its twenty-fifth vessel in your little companion. That means whoever wields it next will be granted immortality."

Mama Dabi's words echoed around the chamber. Every head turned to Zero.

"It's just a rumor," Camih said quickly.

"Lies!" Mama Dabi hissed. "There is nothing I want more in the whole galaxy right now. The universe is vast. The life of a space bandit is dangerous and risky. But with immortality to look forward to, imagine everything I could do? I could sail the galaxy to my heart's content and conquer it all!"

Her eyes glowed with desire and ambition.

"You had an asset like this and you never thought to bring it to the woman who raised you and taught you everything you know, Camih? That is perhaps the greatest disappointment of all. Khabib, bring us the Thorn of Roses and we will start torturing the boy."

"Yes, Mom," said Khabib. He bowed low and left the chamber with the red-haired boy, giving Camih a goading look as he went by.

A few moments later, Khabib returned pushing a strange mechanical device. It looked like a sarcophagus, but the interior was lined with spikes. A clear tube ran from the top of the sarcophagus into a black cube.

"Here is the Kobasticker extractor, Mom," said Khabib, grinning.

Zero's knees shook.

"Good. Now place the boy inside it."

Zero finally found his voice.

"I think that you will be doing yourself a great disservice if you do this," he said.

"Do you now?" purred Mama Dabi, turning her eyes on him.

"I do. Putting me through the Kobasticker extractor might make for some great entertainment, if you are into that sort of thing, but it won't get you Jupiter and it won't get you your immortality."

"You're just trying to save your own life!" accused Khabib.

"I won't deny that. But I don't want you having misconceptions about how Jupiter works."

That made Khabib and Mama Dabi stop in their tracks. The longer he kept them guessing, the longer he would stay alive. He did not look at Ladi or Camih because he was afraid he would lose focus. Thoughts were buzzing through his mind like honeybees.

"Jupiter cannot be forcibly removed," Zero said. "It has to be given willingly."

"You will give it willingly once we've finished with you, trust me," said Khabib.

Zero shook his head.

"Think about it. If all it took to obtain the Jupiter was to torture the previous owner until he gave it up, then it would have been done before. The owners of the Jupiter would have been locked up in prisons and tortured until it had gone through twelve users. In fact, there would be dozens of immortals by now. But there aren't, which means that the strategy doesn't work.

"The Jupiter will only pass to the next user when I will it to. That is how it I got it from its previous user."

That was not exactly true, but Zero didn't care. He was getting comfortable now. Each word left his mouth like a dart finding its target.

"Mom! Don't listen to—"

"Quiet, Khabib. Continue," said Mama Dhabi, nodding at Zero.

"There is a certain task I must carry out, and I need assistance. In exchange for that help, I would perhaps be so generous as to relinquish my claim to the Jupiter," said Zero.

Mama Dhabi's gaze fixed on him now.

"What task are we talking about?" she asked.

Khabib watched as his dream of getting even with Camih receded.

Zero took a breath to compose himself. If he wasn't careful, he would undo the work he had accomplished so far.

"It is an object that once belonged to my employer, and some people are trying to take it for themselves. I mean to stop them."

"What object?"

"The Mask of the Shaman King."

Zero braced himself. Incredibly, there was no flicker of recognition in Mama Dabi's eyes. She either had never heard of the Mask of the Shaman King or didn't know enough about it to understand its power.

"And who are those who are after it? Who are your enemies?"

"Mom, they would have us go to war with the Space Mafia!" pleaded Khabib. "They want to fight against Rozan—"

"Ha!" Mama Dabi crowed. "That little punk. With his father gone, he thinks he is the king of the world. Well, they have it coming to them."

She seemed to ponder Zero's proposal. "How do I know that you speak the truth?" she asked.

"Those who own Jupiter must live by certain moral codes. You'll have to trust me."

The room fell silent.

Zero felt a cool wind blow across the back of his neck. But it might have been his imagination.

"Will you make your pledge here?" asked Mama Dabi.

Zero was aware of Camih's heavy gaze. He stood up straight, held a hand to his heart, and in his most formal voice said:

"I, Zero of the Jupiter, make this pledge to you: Should you assist me in retrieving the Mask of the Shaman King, and should we prevail against Rozan and the Space Mafia, then I promise that I will relinquish my right to the Jupiter."

Mama Dabi smiled slowly. Satisfaction glinted in her eyes.

"Khabib, get them a whizzer ready."

"But Mom!"

"Get these people what they need in terms of ships and a crew. You are to help them retrieve the object they are looking for. But be warned, Zero of the Jupiter," she said, her voice laced with steel, "Nobody plays with Mama Dabi. Should any of you even think about crossing me, I will kill you."

CHAPTER 24

THE trip in Khabib's whizzer could not have been more different the second time around.

Gone were the juvenile jokes and the constant cackling. Gone, too, were the loud hip-hop songs.

Khabib piloted the whizzer, mumbling darkly under his breath. His fellow Scorpiodukes sat in silence, their shoulders hunched and their eyes staring listlessly into space.

Zero was still in disbelief at how he'd managed to convince Mama Dabi to help them retrieve the Mask of the Shaman King. They were on their way to Atchani, the planet they'd seen on the map of the Tear of Kings, with a dozen whizzers from Mama Dabi's fleet to assist them.

Camih, meanwhile, could not stop talking.

"That did not go quite as you had expected, now did it, Khabib?" she goaded.

Khabib growled, his grip tightening on the control wheel.

"You thought you would be rewarded for dragging me back to Mama Dabi, didn't you? How is that working out for you? In the end, you get to follow me, Zero, and Ladi on a mission to retrieve an object from the Space Mafia. Isn't this great?"

Khabib shot her a glare that could have punched a hole through the hull of a ship.

"Somebody's in a bad mood! Where are all the jokes now? Where's the music?" asked Camih.

"What's the plan when we get to Atchani?" asked Khabib, changing the subject.

"A straightforward recovery mission. We determine the location of the Mask and we retrieve it," said Ladi.

"Then we return to Mama Dabi, and your friend gives the Jupiter to Mama Dabi as he promised," finished Khabib.

"That goes without saying!" said Ladi. Zero saw him cross his fingers behind his seat.

"I don't trust you guys. I know that you guys will try to pull off something before this is over with. I can smell it," said Khabib, his eyes narrowing into slits.

Zero was staring out the front window as they approached a small, frost-colored planet.

"The moment we get there, Rozan will be able to read our minds," said Zero. "How are we going to counter that?"

"Leave that to me," said Camih confidently.

In the distance, a large moon was passing across the face of a star.

A *lunar eclipse*, thought Zero, and stared at Camih.

"Are you thinking what I'm thinking?" he said.

"The word 'eclipse' was on the map in the Tear."

"My guess is the eclipse could reveal the resting place of the Mask!" said Zero.

Both Zero and Ladi pointed out the window to where two black dots in space were growing bigger and bigger. As they got closer, they settled into the shapes of black battle whizzers silhouetted by the bright orange of their jet propulsors.

"Black Raptor 3500s, third generation," said Khabib dismissively. "From that distance, they're about as dangerous as dead starfish."

Two beams of light shot toward them, basking the inside of the cockpit in pale blue light.

"You were saying?" growled Zero.

"Don't worry," Khabib drawled. "Even if they hit us, we would only suffer minor damage. This whizzer is coated in reinforced Rodarian steel. Not to mention it does zero to the speed of light in twenty-two seconds, so we could outrun them. It would take at least a fifth-generation Raptor 7300 to make a scratch on this bad b—"

Something struck their side and made the whole whizzer shudder. The cockpit was suddenly plunged into darkness before a red pulsing light filled the cabin. A deafening alarm went off. On the dashboard, the words *Critical Damage* were flashing.

"You were saying?" Zero repeated, shouting.

"Me and my big mouth!" cried Khabib. "Everybody hold on!"

The whizzer lurched forward just as Zero managed to clip on his seat belt.

He noticed the other whizzers in their fleet breaking formation and darting away.

The unlucky crew members who had not strapped themselves into their seats were plastered against the back of the cabin as the spaceship plunged toward Atchani.

A second round of fire struck the whizzer, and the display on the screen changed. The familiar symbol of a skull and crossbones appeared, followed by an animation of a few coffins spinning in a circle.

"That does not look good, bud," Ladi said to Khabib.

Plumes of smoke were coming out of the front of the whizzer and flowing over the windshield, obstructing their vision.

Zero said a silent prayer. Khabib was hunched over the control panel, a frantic look on his face.

"All right, guys, good news!" shouted Khabib over the screeching of the warning system. "It seems like the Raptors have stopped giving chase."

"I wonder why!" screamed Camih sarcastically.

"The bad news is that we are going to hit the surface in five ... four ... three ..."

The impact caused Zero's body to shoot forward with such violence that he thought his limbs might tear off.

The whole cabin became a spinning whirlwind. Zero felt as if he'd been tossed into a giant tumble dryer.

Several crew members were bouncing around the cabin like popped corks.

Zero's head struck the window and he was knocked unconscious.

When he came to, his ears were ringing. The world swam in front of him, his vision blurred.

He was being dragged away from the burning wreckage.

Zero saw Camih pulling out Ladi, her hands hooked under his armpits.

There was a bright flash as the whizzer exploded. Debris

came bursting toward them, missing Zero by only a few inches.

"Zero! Zero, can you hear me?" cried Camih.

Zero focused his gaze on Camih kneeling beside him.

"Is everyone okay?" he asked. It was so cold he could see his breath.

She nodded.

"The snow helped cushion us," said Khabib, answering the question Zero had not had the time to voice. "The rest of our whizzers have flown off, the cowards."

Zero slowly got to his feet and looked around at the crew, battered and bruised but all still standing.

Zero was about to speak when he saw what awaited them. He blanched, slowly raising his hands in the air.

Camih, Ladi, and Khabib followed his gaze.

A small throng of Space Mafia soldiers had their laser guns aimed at them.

They slowly parted as Efua made her way between them.

Her eyes were sparkling with excitement. She was wearing a fur coat, and her breath came out in little clouds of vapor when she spoke.

"You really shouldn't have come here, Zero."

CHAPTER 25

ZERO and the rest of the crew were separated, and their Saba gloves confiscated by Sunday. As they approached an ancient-looking temple, Efua took Camih one way and Sunday took Zero, Ladi, Khabib, and the others down to some dungeons. Sunday seemed the worse for wear since they had last seen him. He now wore a neck brace, had a black eye, and his rhinoceros face was almost entirely covered in bandages. Zero did not hesitate to comment on it, much to Ladi's enjoyment.

"You've got to tell me what you're using on your skin, Sunday. It glows. Let me guess, Essence of Run-over-by-a-Truck with a bit of GBH?" said Zero.

There was a lot of sniggering.

Ladi winked at Zero and mouthed, "Brilliant."

"You'll achieve my look if you don't shut up," growled Sunday.

Zero and the rest of the boys were placed in one big cell that was essentially a natural alcove blocked off by steel bars. Dozens of stalactites speared down from the roof and let droplets of icy water fall into puddles on the floor.

"It's leaking in here, boss. You're not trying to drown us, I hope," said Khabib.

"Quiet! The boss has been looking forward to this moment for a long time. This curse that caused his father to fall into an unending sleep will slowly consume him too. With the Mask of the Shaman King, he will be able to lift his family's curse. My job is to stop you punks from interfering with his plans."

Sunday promptly sat on the floor opposite their cell and opened a copy of *Stargirl* magazine. Next to him, the gang's Saba gloves were stacked in a pile.

Zero rested his head against the bars, the cool, hard touch of metal helping him think. He absently began to knock on the bars with his fists.

Sunday looked up from his magazine and glared at him.

Zero turned to Ladi. For a moment they stood staring at each other. Then Ladi nodded, and pulled a minuscule device from his jacket pocket. He gestured for Khabib and his crew to put their fingers in their ears.

Ladi cleared his throat. "I never thought I would be in the mood to listen to one of Octave's poems, but here goes. This one is called 'Trigonometry under an August Moon.'"

Ladi pushed a button and the sound of Octave's voice reciting his poem filled the room.

Ladi and Zero quickly put their fingers in their ears, blocking out the noise.

The veins in Sunday's brow bulged and his grip tightened on the magazine, crinkling the pages.

After a while he threw his magazine aside and jumped to his feet.

"Will you be quiet!" he bellowed.

The whole room fell silent.

Sunday's glare swept over the cell, but he couldn't spot Ladi's tape recorder. He struck the bars with the heel of his hand.

"Be quiet!" he roared.

Ladi and Zero locked gazes, and Zero nodded imperceptibly.

"*Koba-Jupiter*," said Zero under his breath, just as Sunday slammed his palms against the bars once more.

In his rage, Sunday had failed to notice that Zero had materialized his Kobasticker and pressed it against his right forearm.

Zero pressed his fingers against the metal bars and sent an electric pulse along them just as Sunday made contact with the bars.

Sunday straightened up immediately and his teeth chattered. A small buzzing sound could be heard, like a set of clippers being turned on. His fingers locked around the bars.

Zero walked toward Sunday, his two fingers sliding across a horizontal beam of the cell door. He could see the fear in Sunday's eyes. When he was right in front of him, Zero smiled.

"Having a short temper is a terrible thing. Sunday, here is the situation: I currently have two fingers pressed against these bars. This might sound trivial, but I have a Kobasticker that lets me manipulate electricity. The special thing about my ability is that the strength of the charge I release depends on the number of fingers I use. With two fingers, I can cause your muscles to contract. But if I were to place my third finger like so"—he lightly brushed his third finger against the bar and watched as Sunday's eyes rolled back in his head, his whole body vibrating—"we would be talking a possible heart attack. Now, with four fingers—"

"D-d-don't!" Sunday sputtered.

"Music to my ears."

Ladi searched Sunday's pockets. He found the keys to the cell and pulled them out. The whole time, Sunday's eyes jittered in their sockets.

"Thank you, Sunday," said Zero. He firmly pressed all three fingers against the bars.

There was a flash of light and a *zap* as Sunday was sent crashing back against the wall. He slumped to the ground, unconscious.

A few minutes later, Zero and the rest of the gang were out.

"What do we do now?" asked Khabib.

"We find Rozan. Camih is sure to be with him."

"And how do we know where Rozan is?"

Zero looked toward the sunken figure of Sunday, an idea already forming in his mind.

CHAPTER 26

WITH the threat of further electrocution, Sunday helped the crew recover their weapons and then led them through the temple to Rozan.

The corridors had large square windows through which Zero got a look at the darkening sky.

He felt a stab of panic as he saw that Atchani's sun was now nothing more than a thin, glowing crescent.

They found Rozan on the roof, in the pit of an open-air theater covered in snow. He held the Tears of Kings in his right hand, and next to him were two stone altars—one with a square-shaped depression in it.

A congregation of Space Mafia henchmen formed a circle around their boss.

On Zero's left, Efua emerged, dragging a gagged Camih out of the mouth of a tunnel. Camih stumbled forward, her hands tied behind her back.

"I admire your persistence," said Rozan as Zero and his crew descended the steps toward him.

"Stop what you're doing, or he gets it," said Zero, holding to Sunday's head two fingers that glowed with the Jupiter's energy.

Rozan laughed. It sounded like knives sharpening.

"I think you have a very poor understanding of your hostage's value. Sunday is worth nothing to me."

Sunday let out a whimper.

"Nothing is going to stop me from going through with this. The Namakou's curse robbed me of my father these past eight years. How fitting that I will use one of their treasures to bring him back to me. You must see the beauty in it too."

Rozan lowered the Tear of Kings into the altar cavity.

The sky began to darken further. Zero looked at Efua, who was shepherding Camih toward Rozan.

"Efua!" screamed Zero. "You can't let him do this! He will use you and discard you like he does with everybody!"

His words echoed dully around the theater.

Efua did not react, her expression like the surface of a frozen lake.

"Save your breath," said Rozan.

Zero turned to the rest of the people gathered.

"He's going to kill you all! The Mask of the Shaman King needs souls in order to work. He has brought you all here to *die!*" he cried.

This seemed to carry more weight. A number of heads turned toward Rozan. There was a flutter of unease. They had seen enough of their boss's proclivity for discarding collaborators and allies alike to know that it was a possibility.

Zero felt his body seize up. Every muscle tensed, and a searing pain roared through his brain. He had experienced Rozan's mind-control ability before, but those times had been dress rehearsals by comparison.

The others were all frozen in place—except for Efua.

Rozan's henchmen began to glow with a pale white aura, a strange vapor escaping from their mouths and ears. A few of them collapsed lifelessly.

"The Mask of the Shaman King is in our midst. Its presence is already harvesting lives for its own power."

Zero looked down at his hands and recoiled as the very same vapor began to rise from his hands. Zero felt the world slowly drifting away from him, as if his essence was being tugged out of his body.

Rozan's gaze swept over the bodies of his henchmen.

"They were nothing before the Space Mafia took them in and gave them a future. Their lives belong to me."

The light trickled out of the sky with frightening speed, like the last pinch of sand down an hourglass. The sun was barely visible, its light limning the moon.

A narrow beam of golden light shot through an aperture in the wall behind Rozan and struck the Tear of Kings. It was refracted across the theater, bouncing off the empty stone altar.

A glacial wind blew across the theater, sending snow pelting against Zero's face. Strange, glowing symbols began to appear on the altar, stretching down to the ground and across the temple, lighting up the entire theater.

Slowly, a shape took form atop the altar, shimmering with a bright blue light.

The Mask of the Shaman King.

They'd misunderstood this since the beginning. The symbol on the ground was a giant summoning type Kobasticker that materialized the Mask. It's what made it so hard to find. The Order of Lassa had tried to hide the entire temple floor.

Rozan walked closer to the Mask, the only figure moving in a sea of living statues.

Zero looked across at Efua. Her face was lit by the glow of

the markings on the altar. For one panic-filled moment they stood staring at each other, and then she winked at him.

Zero was stunned. He watched her press two fingers against her forearm.

"*Koba-Blueflash*," she breathed.

A blaze of blue light speared through Rozan's leg. He stumbled against the altar, his face full of confusion and pain as he crumpled to the ground.

Instantly, Rozan's mind-control spell was broken.

Zero felt a painful snap like a rubber band against his skin as the floating fragments of his soul reentered his body.

Rozan looked up at the brightening sky and then roared at Efua, his face rumpled in fury.

"What have you done?" Rozan snarled, gnashing his teeth.

Efua passed a hand across her face. It undulated and rippled like water as she peeled off her "face" in one motion.

Camih stared back at them, grinning, her eyes bright.

Zero glanced at the bound and gagged Camih on the ground and saw Efua's bright green eyes glaring at him.

Camih had used their disguises to switch places!

"Impossible!" cried Rozan.

"I always told you your ego would be your downfall," she purred, stepping closer. "It's harder to use your Kobasticker with the pain clouding your mind, isn't it? And without it, you're useless."

Zero needed to get to the Mask, but he knew that the instant he rushed for it, it would become a free-for-all.

He braced himself and made a run for it.

"Stop!" yelled Khabib. He held a laser gun, its barrel aimed at Zero's heart. "I can't let you do that. Mama Dabi will want that mask. Hands up or I'll shoo—"

Khabib's eyes went cross-eyed. The gun slipped out of his hands as he collapsed on the floor in a heap. Ladi stood behind him, his palm smoking slightly and a Kobasticker glowing on his wrist.

"You talk too much," said Ladi, nudging Khabib's unconscious form.

All hell broke loose. The theater was filled with the flashes of laser gunfire and Kobasticker spells as Zero and Ladi dove toward the Mask. Together, they held off the few henchmen remaining and Khabib's crew.

A cry of pain drew his attention.

Efua had escaped her bindings and was now attacking Camih. Camih was wielding a shield made from purple energy to deflect the red beams of energy Efua was aiming at her. But as she backpedaled, Camih tripped over Khabib's prone body, making her lose focus. Her shield dropped, just for a heartbeat, but Efua's next bolt of energy struck her in the chest.

Camih's whole body went rigid before she collapsed.

Zero screamed her name.

Efua turned to Zero. He saw her palm glow once more as she sent a red beam of energy screaming toward him.

Instinctively, Zero reached out and touched the Mask, just before the beam struck him in the chest too.

CHAPTER 27

ZERO was standing in front of a giant baobab tree, its hulking trunk growing out of the remains of a giant clay building as if it had been hatched from it. The tree rose so high it disappeared into the clouds.

All around him stretched an endless savanna full of brown-and-yellow palettes under a powder blue sky laced with thin clouds.

Zero patted his chest, looking for the wound from Efua's curse, but he was whole.

In front of him appeared a figure made entirely of light. Zero got the vague impression of a young girl, but she was shining so bright he could not look directly at her.

When she spoke, her words materialized inside his mind rather than traveling to his ears.

Welcome, Saba, she said, her voice clear and calm.

"Where am I?"

You are in the Mask of the Shaman King.

"Who are you?"

Afi, daughter of Selima Turkoglu.

Zero swallowed.

"You were sacrificed by King Brabus," he said.

The Mask grants its users their wishes. Tell me your greatest wish, Saba, and it will be accomplished.

Zero thought of Camih.

"My friend . . . Is she going to be okay?"

She will be.

The girl hovered closer to Zero. He had the impression she was sifting through his being and looking through every single thought he had ever had.

I could give you power the likes of which no man has never seen. With it, you could become the greatest Saba ever known. All those who once mocked you would be sorry.

"I don't need that."

I could destroy your enemies. Eradicate the one who hurt your friend and give you victory in your current battle.

"I'm okay, thanks," said Zero, nervous now.

And then Afi said: *I could take you to your parents.*

Zero froze. He imagined the embrace of a mother and father, things the universe had robbed him of.

But he also thought of the consequences. If he used the Mask in this way, he would be breaking the sacred rule of the Sabas by using his role to gratify his own personal desires.

But you would have your mother.

He thought, too, of Mrs. Turkoglu, and the shame he would feel for using the artifact against her people's wishes.

But you would have your mother.

Doubts began to circle his mind like a pack of hyenas around prey.

Zero could feel the power of the Mask coursing through him. It was an intoxicating feeling. With it, he could sense all the endless possibilities at his disposal. Achievements and goals requiring years of work and effort were plucked from their place in a distant, unknowable future and dangled before him.

And then there was something else: a dark presence at the edge of his thoughts. Like a silhouette lurking behind a door.

Zomon—the Dark King.

He could feel Zomon's eagerness building with Zero's weakening resolve. Zomon could almost taste his freedom.

Zero shook his head.

Yes, he would be reunited with his parents. But at what cost?

The thought pierced the haze of power and greed that had settled on his mind. Like ants fighting off an intruder, his positive thoughts grew stronger and chased out the thoughts that had been planted there by the Mask.

"It does sound so easy. But then what would it cost me?"

Nothing.

"But what will it cost others?"

The spirit was silent.

"Even if they are people I do not know, their pain is still real. I would be bending the lives that were used to create this mask to my purpose. Using their sacrifices to fulfill my own desires. I would be encouraging other people to do the same."

If you do not wish to do this, other people will.

"And they will have to live with the consequences of their actions. I know my dreams are hard. But I know that in time I will achieve them, without having to do things I don't agree with."

You will not use our power?

Zero shook his head. "I made a promise to your mother."

There was a change in the air. It felt soft, like walking out of the harsh sun into the shade.

My . . . mother?

The words sounded like wind whistling through tree leaves.

"Your mother has been looking for you. I promised her that I would return the Mask to her so she could perform the ceremony to free your soul. If I were to betray your mother's trust and use the Mask for myself, I know I wouldn't be able to look my own mother in the eye. She would be ashamed of me."

Zero thought he could feel Afi smile, but he could not be sure.

It is time for you to return to your friends, Saba.

Zero had almost forgotten. He still had to fend off Rozan and Efua. Suddenly, using the Mask of the Shaman King did not seem like such a bad idea.

Close your eyes. Place your hands together.

Zero did as he was told. He felt a soft caress against his cheek.

Thank you, Zero.

Before he could even react, he felt himself falling into darkness.

CHAPTER 28

ZERO felt his body began to twitch. Something was surging through his veins.

His eyes flew open as a great pillar of energy shot from his body up into the sky.

Dark clouds streaked with lightning rolled outward from the pillar and raced across the sky. A terrible wind picked up, lashing snow around the theater.

His body churned like he was teeming with angry bees made of pure electricity.

Jupiter glowed on his arm, and he watched transfixed as it seemed to change shape, the familiar circle thinned out and a symbol formed a centaur holding a lightning bolt. Then it was gone.

Do not panic, Zero, Afi's voice whispered. *What you feel is the power of the Mask. I will help you. You must take your friends to safety.*

Rozan was slowly getting to his feet, his leg still wounded and bleeding.

Khabib had regained consciousness and taken one look at Zero's surging power before bolting for the exit, his crew at his heels.

Zero turned and looked at Efua, rage at her betrayal boiling within him.

Jupiter glowed on his arm.

There was the loud crack of thunder followed by a brilliant flash of lightning. And for a brief moment the ground was lit up with little squares of light, like a chessboard. The pattern of dark and light squares appeared for a moment and then disappeared.

Gripping the Mask in his hands, Zero spoke, his voice like the echo of thunder in a cave.

"Walk on the light spots and you will be safe. Walk on the squares of darkness and you will be struck down by lightning."

Rozan laughed but it lacked conviction.

Sirens wailed in the distance—the Space Force.

"Zero!" cried Ladi. "We have to go!"

Zero struggled to reel in his power. It was a surging, roiling mass inside him.

"Zero!" Camih shouted. She was injured, pressing a scrap of cloth to her chest, but she was alive. "Zero, it's time to go home!"

Home.

And as dozens of Space Force patrol cars landed on the roof of the temple, Zero emitted a final flash of lightning and portaled the three of them home.

CHAPTER 29

ZERO came to in Shango Heart's hospital wing.

Ladi filled him in on everything that had happened on Atchani.

Apparently, Zero had whisked them back to the guild and then passed out, still holding the Mask. The members of the Space Force had arrived soon after, Inspector Priya in tow.

"We've been cleared. A member of the Space Mafia was arrested in connection with the murder. His Kobasticker matched the signature of the one used to kill the informer."

"What about Camih?"

The events of the past few hours came back to him in spurts. He relived the scene of Camih being shot by Efua and his stomach flipped over.

"She's fine. She's in another room. Just focus on getting better right now."

Zero spent four more days in the clinic, healing from a few broken ribs, some bruises, and exhaustion. It seemed like the Mask of the Shaman King had depleted his Koba reserves. The doctor said it was a miracle he had not lost the ability to use Koba completely.

Every day, someone from Shango Heart came to see him, and it became a ritual Zero learned to look forward to. Of course, Ladi came every day and would bring him the day's newspaper as well as news on the latest Saba rankings.

Even Halima came to see him. She tried to sign him up for an experiment for a new transformation Kobasticker she was designing that could turn you into a space squid for a day, but Zero respectfully declined.

Biscotte the invisible dog came too, and almost single-handedly suffocated him to death with licks. It was rather hard to fend off licks from a dog you could not see.

Even Soraya came by to see him one day with Ladi. But Mr. Gauche was perhaps his favorite visitor. He arrived with a bunch of chocolates and a beautiful marquetry box.

But the whole time, all Zero could think about was Camih. When he was finally discharged on the fourth day, he couldn't wait to see her.

Mr. Gauche organized a huge party. Disco balls were installed around the guild and a Zilbat DJ was hired for the music. Thanks to his eight arms, he could scratch several records at once, and he played an amazing mix of hip-hop and Amapiano songs, which everybody danced to.

Everyone was keen to have a piece of Zero's time. When he finally managed to get some time alone, he sat down at the end of the dining hall and watched the rest of the guild dance.

He looked down at his glass of frozen hibiscus juice and sighed deeply.

Someone tapped his shoulder.

"Hey," said Camih.

She was wearing jeans and a T-shirt with her signature grin. He jumped to his feet and nearly spilled his drink.

Camih smiled.

"You haven't changed, Zero," she laughed. "Still clumsy. How do you feel?"

"Good, I guess." He looked down at his hands. "So much has happened. I'm really glad we could fulfill the mission Zoe left for us . . ."

"But . . . ?" she prodded.

"I miss Zoe. I wish we could somehow find out where she is."

And for a moment, it was as if they'd swept away a rug they had used to disguise the huge hole created by Zoe's absence and it was now laid bare before them.

"I know how you feel, Zero. We'll find her, I promise."

Camih looked at him affectionately. "Come with me, I want to show you something."

Camih led him all the way to the library's mahogany double doors. She held them open for Zero and stepped through.

"I realized I never quite thanked you for saving me."

"I think we're pretty much even. But tell me: How did you manage to swap with Efua?"

Camih smiled.

"The fact is that I never quite trusted Efua from the beginning, so after we bought our disguises, I went and made another based on her and myself. Zoe always said to be prepared for anything. So when she took me hostage, I overpowered her. I took her appearance and made her take mine."

"That's brilliant."

"Right back at you. I saw how you saved us with Mama Dabi. You have no idea how difficult that is. She is very suspicious and almost impossible to swindle."

Zero looked away. He could feel the heat rising to his face.

"What happened to Efua?" asked Zero.

"We don't know. Rozan and any remaining members of his gang were arrested, but no one found Efua."

"And the Mask?"

"Safely returned to Mrs. Turkoglu. She promised to hire lawyers and to lobby for us so we don't get fined for property damage on Atchani."

She took his arm. "Come. I have something to show you."

She pulled him toward a table pushed against the window. Zero could see a large swath of space, dotted with stars.

On the table was a large rectangular object hidden under a black cloth.

"I just want to tell you that I am very proud of you for your progress as a Sabin, Zero. I spoke to Mr. Gauche and he agreed that you have represented the values Shango Heart stands for and are one of the most talented Sabins we have ever had. We think you are ready to go on higher-level missions. But to do that you are going to need this."

She reached out and yanked back the cloth.

In a glass box, lying on a purple cushion, was a genuine Saba Organization membership card.

Zero stared at the gold-plated card, his heart soaring. His name was engraved just above the Shango Heart emblem carved in the center. Underneath the emblem were two stars.

"Congratulations, Zero. For helping to find the Mask of the

Shaman King you have been awarded a two-star rating. It means you show enormous promise—"

The door to the library burst open and Mr. Gauche, Ladi, Octave, and a slew of guild members poured in.

Mr. Gauche beamed at him. "You passed your Sabinhood with flying colors, Zero my lad. It would be an honor for us if you would make our guild your home."

"Congratulations, Zero!" cried Ladi and Octave.

Zero felt a burn in the back of his throat, and his eyes welled up with tears. Camih and Ladi immediately squashed him in a gigantic hug.

Mr. Gauche asked for some music to be played, and some food was brought from the dining hall.

And that was how Zero spent his first evening as an official Saba: surrounded by his family, a member of the greatest guild in the galaxy.

ACKNOWLEDGMENTS

Children of Stardust has been an incredible journey, from the first ideas to the finished manuscript.

I would first like to thank my agent, Sarah Odedina, and Deborah Ahenkorah, cofounders of Accord Literary, for believing in my ideas and for the incredible work they are doing with their team.

Tilda Johnson, editor at Accord, for the invaluable advice and for helping make the story the best it could be.

I want to thank Kristin Allard, my editor at W. W. Norton, and the fantastic team at Norton Young Readers for bringing the world of *Children of Stardust* to life.

And thanks, too, to Abelle Hayford for the wonderful cover and character designs and for bringing the ideas in my head to life.

A number of friends provided me with an incredible amount support during the writing process. I would be remiss if I didn't shout them out:

Kolapo, thank you for being there. Thank you for the long talks. Thank you for helping me put things in perspective whenever I felt I was adrift at sea.

Elyan, my accountability buddy, thank you for keeping me on track! Without us committing to our little system of streaks (however imperfectly) I don't think any writing would have been accomplished. The geekaloos would have remained figments of my imagination and there certainly would not have been any Goobers.

Camih, thank you for the support and for bringing some

good humor in my life when I sometimes had the low spirits of a constipated starfish (which was quite often).

Tami, thank you for listening to me talk for hours on end about a system of magic-infused stickers called Kobastickers. Thank you for our long, geeky discussions about magic, books, films, and role-playing games.

Cesario, Emma, Ursula, Anais, Mayigan, Abla, Daniel, Eli, and all the friends who from near or afar supported me through the great times and the not-so-great times. You made me smile and kept me grounded; your support was precious and appreciated. You created an environment and a bubble of safety that allowed me to write and get my ideas out into the world, despite everything going on around me.

A big thanks to the artist and illustrator Sena Ahadji. You set in motion a series of events that led to me being able to share my stories with the world. You showed me a piece of string poking out from a crack in the wall. I tugged on it and all these incredible things came tumbling into my life

I would also like to take the opportunity to thank all my English teachers throughout the years: Mr. Allen, Ms. Fuchs, and all the others. They lit a passion for writing in my belly and gave me books that were portals into new worlds. And now I am creating my own. They gave me the desire to write, which brings me so much joy and serenity and which I could not live without. For that I can never thank them enough.

ABOUT THE AUTHOR

EDUDZI ADODO was born in Switzerland and raised in Togo. He graduated from Durham University in England, where he studied politics, philosophy, and economics. Now, he writes the stories he wished he'd had as a child: science fiction infused with African culture and mythology. "As Black people and as Africans, what is behind us is so traumatic," he says. "What is around us is too, when you look at issues like police brutality and the rise of intolerance. So why not be forward-looking? Why not anchor ourselves in the future, use that as a starting point, and work backward from there? So I had the idea of writing a space story."

Outside of writing, his passions are basketball, Le Tour de France, manga, and Liverpool Football Club. Edu lives in Lomé, Togo, with his cats, Bijou and Minuit.

ABOUT ACCORD BOOKS

ACCORD works with authors from across the African continent to provide support throughout the writing process and secure regional and international publishing and distribution for their works. We believe that stories are both life-affirming and life-enhancing, and want to see a world where all children are delighted and enriched by incredible stories written by African authors.